TURN THE FUCKING PAGE!!

People are dead, Blake is distraught, and Nina is on the run!

Anabelle Strayer is normally very good at her job as a US Marshal but what happens when she meets someone she just can't get off her mind? Her loyalty and duties as an officer are called into question... as she falls under the enigmatic charms of a beautiful woman while trying to keep a steady relationship with her kind of boyfriend. A boyfriend who has some secrets of his own. Will his revelation help Ana get a grip on reality before anyone else loses their life?

Nina's search and sacrifices for love have forced her to take fate into her own hands as she flees for her life. She narrowly escapes capture from a ruthless gangster who's fixated on making her a prostitute. Taking the risks to secure her freedom from sexual servitude provides an alluring opportunity for Nina to tamper with the investigation dedicated to bringing her in.

Follow Nina as she twists and turns Ana's world upside down while Ana fights to keep herself from falling apart.
See how it all unfolds

***

ISBN: 0991105532

ISBN-13: 978-0-9911055-3-3

Edited by Progressive Edits

Cover Photography: Owen Duckett Jr.

Make-Up: Reginald Raphael

Models: Doug Brinson Jr, Lidia Ornero, & Sandy Soldano

Printed in the United States of America

20 19 18 17 16 15 14 13 12 11 10 9 8 7

Keep Fucking Reading

It's a great fucking story...

We Promise

Loving Nina

T.N. Jones

Phoenix Jones Publishing LLC® | New York

Chapter 1

Most days start the same for Anabelle. She wakes up, hits the snooze on her alarm clock, and turns over to see who's lying beside her. Her long, lusciously soft, crimson red curls cover her face and most of her pillow. She moans as she moves her hair out of the way and lifts the pillow off of the gentleman's head. He's still fast asleep. Her big blue eyes squint trying to narrow her vision. Her mind begins to race and her heart beats rapidly as she tries to remember who the guy is lying next to her. She lifts the top sheet up just enough to glance underneath. His legs are hairy and his penis is huge in its morning state. She struggles through her hangover, trying to remember last night. Anabelle lets the sheet waft to the floor as she gets out of bed.She stumbles into the bathroom wearing only a thin tank top, no bra and no panties. She's disoriented and wondering what her best option is to get this man out of her house. Ana looks at the tall closet next to her sink which hides her badge and firearms. She opens the door, unlocks her gun safe, tosses the holster over her head like a sash and slides her nine millimeter Glock into its favorite place. She grabs a hair tie from around the door knob and throws her hair up into a messy ponytail.

Anabelle stares into her reflection wondering how she let her love life get so cluttered. She can still smell and taste the alcohol from last night. It seems to be seeping from her pores. She watches the man sleeping in her bed through the mirror. Last night's events were so blurry she's still straining to remember who the stranger in her bed is. She walks out of the bathroom stopping at the foot of the bed. She extends her leg out and proceeds to kick and shake the mattress. When the man gets aggravated, he sits up and she draws her weapon. He makes a face of irritation but doesn't react to the firearm.

"Ana, I told you before if you're going to pull that thing out every time this happens you need to stop drinking so heavy," the man responds to the barrel of the gun staring him in the face.

Ana is silent for a moment, while her mind fights with the hangover looming over her like a dark cloud. Finally, it clicks. She holsters her weapon and looks at the man, "I'm sorry Wren." Memories of her attending happy hour with her partner and some of the other agents are slowly coming back to her. Every time she drinks too much, this is the guy she always calls. This is the guy who always comes.

"I forgot who you were for a moment," she offers up the poor excuse for her behavior.

"Ana, I never have a problem coming to get you to take you home. But the drunk wrestling to get me to stay and the escapades that usually follow aren't exactly worth the gun being pointed at me every time I spend the night. Don't get me wrong I love whatever this situation is with us, but you should only pull your weapon if you intend on shooting it."

"You're right and I apologize. I was so hammered last night I barely remember calling you to come get me. My head is pounding, I don't remember where my car is and I gotta get ready for work."

She walks into the bathroom placing the holster and her weapon back into the closet, sheds her tank top and turns on the shower. She wastes no time hopping in to wash off the stench of her embarrassment from this morning's events along with the liquor from last night.

All Wren can do is shake his head as he watches Ana disappear into the bathroom. He begins to rummage through the sheets in search for his clothes. He pulls his boxers and T-shirt out from near the bottom of the bed and stands to put them on. Ana's house was always coldest in the morning, especially in the kitchen which is where he was heading. He returns with two pain killers and his "sure fire" cure for hangovers. He leaves a full glass of a greenish brown liquid sitting on her sink next to the shower. Ana hears movement in the bathroom so she swipes her hand across the glassed-in shower enclosure to see what he is doing. She looks at the gunk sitting in the glass and then to him with a questioning stare.

Right on cue, as if he can read her mind, "Yes you have to drink this crap. You need to function, and I need to get you to work; which is where you left your car by the way." He shows her the two pills before putting them down next to the glass.

"What's in that again?" she asks him with a sour puss still sprawled across her face.

"Espresso, Red Bull and Gatorade... the sure fire way to get rid of any hangover. It doesn't taste as bad as it looks," he tries reasoning with her.

"Yeah, it probably tastes worse!" she exclaims with a laugh.

"Just drink it, pop the pills and finish getting ready. I don't want you to be late for work," he commands while walking out of the bathroom.

Ana finally gets out of the shower. She downs the sludge with the two aspirin, gets dressed, and grabs her badge, gun and duffel bag before heading out to Wren's car.

He was sitting outside with the motor running like they had just pulled off a heist. She laughs at the thought while walking to the car. The morning air is crisp and cold which helps sober her up. Her tequila induced headache starts to subside as the elixir she drank begins to kick in. She gets into the front passenger seat, buckles her seatbelt and proceeds to scroll through her phone notifications while he pulls off into the morning traffic. She has five missed calls and a voicemail from her sister Anna Lee.

Mrs. Strayer had long ago anointed Anabelle as protector and guardian, seeing as she is the eldest of the three sisters. Anastasia is the middle sister, who in her late twenties, still requires Anabelle's rescuing time and time again. She's been in and out of trouble practically her whole life. Always with a yearning desire to find her niche whether it be akin to the responsibility her older sister had, or the attention her baby sister commanded. Her destructive, attention seeking behavior only intensified when their father suddenly passed away while they were teenagers. Anabelle has been saving her ever since. Or at least trying to. The baby, Anna Lee (no longer a Strayer), is in her early twenties, married with a beautiful little girl, Bella, who brings delight and joy everywhere she goes. If only Anna Lee could see that as she is so often infatuated with the idea of her husband dishonoring their vows. So every few weeks or so, she concocts some scheme to catch him in the act, and these schemes usually involve Anabelle using her position, as a U.S. Marshal, to gather "intelligence." Ana loves her sisters without question, but their problems often seep into her work.

She listens to Anna Lee's hyper voicemail message pleading with her to call her back as soon as she gets into the office. Her no-good husband is up to something again. She can just feel it!

Anabelle laughs at the phone as she deletes the message. Wren takes his eyes off the road for a moment to see what she's laughing at. He wants to laugh too, but something in his mind makes him wonder if it was another guy on her phone making her laugh like that. He is very protective, or possessive rather, over the women he cares about. She looks at him, but he turns to focus back on his driving. She leans back in her chair contemplating if she should open up to him. She doesn't move to look at him, but says, "You know sisters can be so funny."

"Oh yeah?," he responds with relief, "I didn't know you had any sisters."

"Yeah I have two, I'm the oldest. And because of my job they call me for a lot of favors. But the antics that they get into are just ridiculous."

"I can only imagine, with you being a Marshal, what kind of favors they're asking you for," he chuckles lightly.

A few minutes later, they're pulling up to the Federal Building where Ana works. Just as she exits Wren's car, her partner, Greg McKinley, drives up behind her in a blue Mazda with his wife, Sharron, in the passenger seat. Both he and Sharron get out of the car so she can get into the driver's seat and he can go into work. Greg is tall and fit with his hair dark brown, square jaw, and hazel eyes. Always donning a polo T-shirt and jeans; he looks like a cop. He bends down to kiss his petite wife as they cross paths.

Ana calls out a quick hello to Sharron who responds with a half-smile. All Ana can do is shake her head. She waves a thank you to Wren and he pulls off in his car.

Greg walks up beside her, "Well good morning Miss Strayer. How are we feeling this morning?" he questions her sarcastically, fully aware of the hangover she should have after all the liquor she consumed the night before.

"We are feeling like shit this morning Mr. McKinley, how about you?" she replies with a chuckle at the truth.

"Could be better, could be worse, but either way I won't complain."

"That's what I like about you Greg, you never complain about anything. Not even when your wife is being a bitch," she states taking a crack at Sharron's snub from a few moments ago.

"Don't start Ana," he warns as they walk into the building and through security.

"But…I mean…I understand that she doesn't like me. But why? I have no idea. You and I been partners for damn near five years now! Why hasn't she gotten used to me, at least to the point where she can fake a few pleasantries?"

"Now Ana, you know why she doesn't like you. Ever since we became partners, she's thought we have a thing going on," Greg says reminiscing of the day his wife met his partner. It was truly a brief introduction, but it was at a bar, during one of their department's happy hour events. Ana had been pounding them down all night. She was getting very flirtatious with all the guys there, even the ones with dates and *wives*. She had made many enemies that night…his wife being the president of that fan club. "She can't stand you even though you're not my type," he informs her.

"Not your type?," Ana asserts with a roll of her eyes. Ana knows that she may not be some Victoria Secret model, but she was definitely not ugly. She has never run into a problem snagging a prize for the night. She has never met a man to tell her no. Her height topping out at five six makes her comfortable for both short and tall men to be with. Her crimson red curls were unnaturally natural with their hues of brown, maroon and burgundy often finding themselves stuffed in a bun while she is working, but unleashed down her back when she's ready to let loose. Those hypnotizing big blues are the color of the sky with a few hints of grey. Her figure is impeccable, although very slim, her womanly curves stand out as ample and very well proportioned to her slender frame. She looks to her partner with all sincerity and cockiness to claim, "Please Greg, I'm everybody's type."

"Exactly, whore isn't my type," he insults her with a smile. Now to anyone on the outside of this partnership, things may seem a bit crass and rude. However, to Ana and Greg, this is the way they function with each other. They both erupt in laughter at his whore comment.

"Oh Greg! I needed that. Even though laughing isn't exactly helping this pain throbbing against my skull," she giggles as they head toward the elevators.

"Well I saw Wren drop you off again, he didn't give you his cure?"

"Yeah I drank the gunk, but it hasn't fully kicked in yet," she mentions while getting off the elevator walking to their offices.

"Aww poor 'I can't handle my liquor and got a headache' baby," he teases her in a voice mimicking a whining toddler. "You need to shape up or don't drink so much. Word around town is we're getting put back into the field together."

"Wait! When did you hear this?" Ana says in astonishment. The last time they were on assignment together, she got into a physical altercation with their target. The target broke her arm and two of her ribs, before he was taken into custody. It took months of required re-training, and physical therapy for her to get cleared for field duty. She's anxious to get off the desk she had been sitting behind. She hits Greg in the shoulder, "Seriously, tell me when did you hear this? Who told you?"

"I did," their commander interjects. The commander is a tall African-American male, with flawless dark chocolate skin. Ana often wondered how it would feel to be taken into his strong arms and pounded into submission but the ring on his left hand and undying devotion to his family usually put those thoughts to rest. *But it never hurt to look*, Ana reasons to herself. The three of them walk into Ana's office. The commander slaps a new file down on her desk. Greg opens it immediately thumbing through the papers, while Ana stands there waiting to hear more about the assignment. She loves the sound of his voice; it's deep and stays with you long after he finishes speaking.

"There's a little metropolis not too far outside of Yonkers, where a Detective Flynn has been working a case, for a little over three months now. He needs our help. The suspect was never in custody but is wanted for at least two counts of murder in the first degree, one count of kidnapping, and attempted murder. However, Flynn feels like she jumped the country already which is way out of his jurisdiction. That's where you two come in."

"So you want us to serve the arrest warrant and bring her in?" Greg asks, never taking his eyes off the paperwork.

"That's exactly what I want you to do. Something in the nature of her crimes says that she's gonna be hard to handle and most definitely hard to catch. Flynn has a few favors owed to him which is why we're being brought in so soon. I want you guys to be careful, especially you Ana. Head out there and give him a hand. Don't come back in here until Nina Slade is in handcuffs." The commander walks out of Ana's office leaving them to their jobs.

"Especially you Ana," Ana mimics the commander's baritone voice, "What the fuck did he mean by that?" She suddenly loses her lust for him.

"I assume he meant that since you got severely hurt on our last assignment you should take extra precautions when we begin to pursue this Slade woman," Greg answers her with a smile full of sarcasm.

"Oh shut up Fucktard!! I knew that, he didn't have to say it though," her voice drops to barely above a whisper with the last few words.

Greg rolls his eyes at her petty grievance and continues to go through the files that he was beginning to spread across her desk.

This is the way they worked. He would do the initial sweep of data so they have a spot to begin and she would add on as the investigation continued. But first, she has to call her sister back. She asks Greg to give her a moment alone to do just that. He walks out of her office to start his routine of grabbing coffee and a muffin from the café, a few floors down.

"Lee, it's Belle. I got your message, I'm at work an—," before Ana can finish leaving her a message, the call waiting is beeping. She clicks over to take the call. "This is Strayer."

"Hey Belle, it's me Lee."

"What happened now Sissy?"

"It's Jason. What else is new? He came home at two-thirty in the morning last night. He stunk of cheap perfume, there was lipstick on his shirt and he was drunk!"

"That sounds a lot like what I did last night," Ana laughs to her sister.

"Anabelle this isn't funny!!" Anna Lee always calls her sister by her whole name to get her attention.

"Sheesh! Okay, okay, okay...what's so wrong about that, Lee? What did he say he was doing when you asked him why he came home in that state?"

"He said a couple of guys from work through his boss a bachelor party that he was mandated to attend! I don't believe him!"

"You never believe him Lee. What do you want me to do?" Ana questions the legitimacy of her sister's frantic state.

"Do what you always do! Check it out and get back to me," Lee commands.

"Actually, I'm going back in the field today so I may not have time to get back to you as soon as I used to but I'll definitely take a look into it Sissy."

"Thanks Sissy. And see if you can find Asia while you're at it," Anna Lee throws in another task for Ana to complete.

"What do you mean… FIND… Asia?" Ana questions, with her elbow propped up allowing her temples to rest between her thumb and fingertips.

"She was at Mommy's house last night causing a ruckus, so Mommy called the cops and told her she had to leave. Asia left before the cops got there and no one knows where she went. You can find her, you always do."

"Sissy, I told you I'm going back in the field today. I don't have time to play find the junkie," Ana growls the response to her sister's request.

"Anabelle, that isn't nice! You know what kind of shit she can get into and you better not let anything bad happen to her! Mommy will die of heartache if anything happens to her because we didn't do anything to save our Anastasia!"

You mean I didn't do anything to save her, she corrects her sister in her mind but decides not to start that argument again right now. Somehow it was always translated that when Anastasia was found, both sisters were to be credited. All Anna Lee does is call to put in the requests, she's never there to pick up the broken pieces of Asia once she's found.

However, Anna Lee always had the right words to get her sisters to do anything she wanted them to. Her wordplay often worked with Anastasia as well, but she had to be located first. She continues to badger her sister over the phone until Ana agrees.

"Okay Lee, I'll put the word out for PD to look for Asia and to just call me if and when they find her but not to book her. I'll have to work on Jason after I get off but I'll look into him too. But I'm sure everything is fine, nothing ever turns up. Stop being so paranoid and just enjoy being married."

"I do enjoy being married Sissy, and you would too. Let me set you up again. I promise this next one will be better," Anna Lee offers her sister.

"No thanks Sissy. There was nothing wrong with the last guy; I just don't have the time or patience to settle down right now. Besides I'm having fun with Wren. He's a no muss no fuss kind of guy, and I like that."

"That guy from physical therapy? You're still messing around with him?"

"Yeah, but Sissy I gotta go. I actually have work to do today," Ana tries to rush her sister off the line.

"I know Belle. I'll let you go. And Sissy…"

"Yes Lee?"

"Congratulations on getting back into the field. I know how hard you've been working to get passed what happened and I'm proud of you. Love you, talk to you soon," Anna Lee hangs up the receiver just as Ana utters an "I love you," in return.

Right on cue, Greg comes into her office with an extra cup of coffee and sits it on her desk. He sees the look on her face. "Your sisters again?"

"Yeah, you know it. An Ana's job is never done," she answers wondering when she was going to find the time to do everything Lee asked her to do.

"Well don't worry about them now. We gotta go see Flynn and get a handle on this case."

Anabelle agrees, finally getting up from her chair. She takes a sip of the hot coffee and packs up all the paperwork on her desk. She follows Greg to the parking garage where her car is parked from the night before. They drive for a little over an hour to the 128th Precinct where they meet Detective Flynn.

Detective Flynn is noticeably exhausted and explains to Greg and Ana that he's been searching high and low for Nina, but to no avail. Her fingerprints aren't in the system and the prints they do have can't be matched until she's brought in. There has been so much death associated with this one woman, and he's desperate to bring her in. He scrolls through all of his notes on the investigation and then sits back quietly while they match his paperwork up with their own.

Ana finally looks up from her notes and at the detective, "So what makes you think she's left the country?"

"Well," Detective Flynn begins to explain, "Call it a hunch; but that Xavier guy disappeared. She and the Dalton guy, who she shot and killed, were gathering information against Xavier. I just find it too coincidental they up and vanished around the same time. His passport was tagged leaving the country and so was hers but somehow I can't find what country they landed in. It's like I lost them midair."

He's right though he can't prove it. Nina and Xavier paid some flight crew personnel to swap their passports once they were in the air. The person checking the boarding passes checked them in and two extra passengers under their aliases. So when the plane landed their aliases walked off while Nina and Xavier were lost en route.

"Were they on the same flight out of the same airport?" Greg asks.

"Well no, but they both left within a few days of each other," Flynn answers.

"So maybe...she's just a psychopath who fled and he's a million-dollar-embezzling coward. That doesn't mean they were in on it together. Especially since they didn't leave together, they weren't on the same flight and you don't know where either of them actually went," Ana reasons.

"That's true but my gut is telling me that they're together. And that's why you guys are here! To find out where the hell they went and bring them back in!"

"Our mission right now is bringing Nina in, and if we catch a break maybe we'll get to this Xavier guy as well, but thanks Detective. We'll be in touch if we need anything else from you," Greg assures him as he stands up extending his hand out to him. Ana stands from her seat as well, waves and exits the precinct without saying much. Her hangover is still bothering her but not as much as earlier.

She waits outside in the cool air for Greg to come out of the police station. He has decided to call Miss Redwood to let her know they were on their way to talk with her about what happened with Nina.

The drive to Blake's house isn't that far from the station. When they reach the front gate, it's wide open. There are a few guys making repairs to the iron. No one stops Ana from driving onto the property, and no one speaks to them through the intercom. All Ana and Greg hear are the sounds of the men welding the iron. They drive up the driveway and stop at the front steps.

Eileen, Blake's assistant, is standing outside at the top of the stairs waiting to greet them. Ana and Greg get out of her car and walk up the stairs. They show Eileen their badges and she escorts them inside.

Eileen offers them a seat in the kitchen telling them that Blake will be downstairs momentarily to answer whatever questions she needs to.

When Blake makes her way into the kitchen, she is less than presentable. Her hair is messy, thrown into a sloppy bun, her clothes are a bit dingy as if she hasn't changed them in days and her eyes are bloodshot red as if she hasn't slept in weeks.

"How can I help you officers today?" Blake asks. Her voice is barely above a whisper and full of exhaustion.

"Well Miss Redwood, we just want to get your perspective of what took place at your office about three months ago," Greg responded to her solemnly.

"I told the cops this story a million times already. That bitch I gave birth to went fucking nuts and started killing people, or having people killed. The story she told me about why she did it and what happened was so long and drawn out I don't remember all of the details. What I remember is the look on Benjamin's face right before the bullet went into his forehead. What I remember is being talked into going with that psychopath because she told me Benjamin was in danger and would be killed if I didn't. And he died anyway! She killed him anyway! And Darren was shot too! I was responsible for her and I gave her away, so she did this to me!" Blake can feel herself tearing up, as the moments from that day begin to replay over and over again in her head. Blake is immediately remorseful for having agreed to do this meeting today.

Ana moves off of her stool and walks over to Blake. Her blame and sadness reminded her of her sister, Anastasia and one of her mood swings. She immediately begins to console her, "I know it must be hard living with what happened day after day. We apologize for making you go through this all over again but we really want to make sure we catch Nina, before she changes her mind about letting you live."

Greg slaps his forehead eyeing Ana wildly. Ana was great at times, but barely tolerates people and their emotions which makes her a bit abrupt. He imagines dealing with her sisters all of the time made her this way. He tries to clean up what Ana crassly suggested, "Yes we want to catch Nina because we know how dangerous she might be. And any information you might be able to give us, maybe an insignificant detail that you might have forgotten to tell the police…something that you didn't think was important or that may have seemed odd to you."

Blake sucks up her tears and thinks for a moment. "The only thing that I can think of is the security guard in the lobby didn't call the cops. He was there when I walked in with Nina, but I had to go downstairs to let the police into the building after everything happened. I think I told the detective but it was a while ago, so I'm not sure."

"Okay, Blake thank you for your time. I'm pretty sure that any other information we need from you is in the reports but we appreciate you taking the time out to talk to us," Ana rubs the top of her hand lightly.

"Yes thank you," Greg says standing from his stool. "We'll definitely be in touch."

Blake follows Greg and Ana out of the kitchen to her front door. They thank her again and step out into the autumn air. Ana walks over to the driver's side and gets into the car. Greg gets in and they sit there for a moment trying to decide where they should go next. They begin sorting through the files they have trying to find out the information on the security guard and why he never called the police that evening. Ana finally finds his information scribbled across the top of a page along with an eight digit number next to his name. It was too long to be a phone number, so it had to be some other identifier. After making a few calls they discover that the guard was arrested some weeks ago. So their next destination is county lockup.

Ana is full of excitement and anxiety as her first full day in the field is proving to be one of her busiest. They drive back toward the center of the city, hoping to make it to the jail quickly. The entire trip there, all Ana and Greg can think about is, *Where the hell is Nina Slade?*

Chapter 2

The sand is velvety soft as Nina buries her toes beneath its surface.

The sun has barely risen and the beach is just beginning to warm up.

The melody from tropical birds singing in the background, makes

her swoon under the morning sky. The air is crisp as she inhales the

scent of the clear seawater crashing upon the shore. She leans back

in the wooden beach chair, basking in the morning sunrise. She hears

someone approaching from behind her and knows its Xavier coming

to bring her breakfast. He gets up close and is standing in front of her

blocking the sunlight and warmth. He reaches down for her hand and

begins to pull it trying to get her up out of the seat.

"Come on Nina! I need you to get up," he frantically whispers to her.

Her face is full of bewilderment, as she stays in her seat refusing to budge.

"Come on Nina! Get up! Where's the rest of the money?" Xavier raises his voice.

"What money? What are you talking about?" she whines turning over onto her side to face the wall.

"Nina, wake up!" Xavier shakes her out of her dreams jolting her back into reality.

"What the fuck?" she shouts trying to stop the vigorous movement of her body.

Nina wakes from her tropical escape to the cold, closet sized room she and Xavier have been staying in for the last few weeks.

"Nina, I'm sorry baby but I really need the rest of the money," Xavier's piercing blue eyes stare down into hers until she fully awakens. His black hair, streaked with touches of grey, is slicked back with a few unruly strands falling in his face. His beard is beginning to grow in. Nina sits up in the small bed and looks around disappointed wishing she were in the warm climate of her dreams.

"What's going on?" she asks getting up searching around for clothes to put on.

"I owe Gabriel twenty, and the money we have in the safe isn't enough to give those guys downstairs. So where's the rest of it? I know we have more," Xavier can feel the panic beginning to settle in. He knows he only has a few more minutes before Gabriel's boys take the hike up the stairs to their small studio apartment. If they come up, he knows things aren't going to go well for either of them.

"Really? Again Zay? You let that crook take you for another twenty thousand dollars? I can't believe you! We're supposed to be living off this cash and you just keep gambling it away. There's only six left in the safe, and you know I have to go back to the States to get some more," Nina reminds him.

Xavier can hear the disappointment and aggravation in her tone, "I had a pair of Aces! There's no reason I should have lost. And why didn't you move the money to a Swiss Bank or Cayman Island account? Why are you willing to risk going back into the U.S.? I knew I should have managed all of the money."

"If we left it up to you…you'd gamble the entirety of it! I can't believe you thought you could win twenty thousand off a card shark! Why are you so stupid when it comes to poker? And I didn't have time to move the money remember? Under the circumstances I say getting us out of the country was more important than moving the money and having it seized by the authorities. I can't believe you have to pay this asshole again! You just gave him fifteen last week! Hasn't it dawned on you that he lets you win smaller pots so he can take you in the bigger ones?" Nina tries to reason with him.

"Shit! They're coming...okay we can talk about this later. Grab whatever you can and let's get the hell out of here," Xavier exclaims grabbing important papers off of a desk. He moves to the safe next, grabbing everything out of it. Nina throws on a few extra layers of clothing. She looks at him moving around the room at lightning speed. Then Xavier moves toward the window. He unlocks it and lifts the rickety wooden pane allowing the freezing wind to whip inside the apartment. The Moscow night air is crisp as he steps out of the window onto the fire escape. He looks to Nina motioning for her to come with him. She shakes her head in disbelief not wanting to climb out of the window.

"Get your ass over here!" Xavier yells through his teeth just as three solid knocks bang on the front door. A heavily accented voice booms from the other side, "Jared! You are taking too long. Open the door and let's get this over with!"

That voice is just the motivation Nina needs to get her ass out of the third story window. The wind is whirring and slapping her in the face with freshly fallen snow. It turns her cheeks red as she steps out onto the fire escape. She shuts the window behind her. Xavier is halfway down to the second level when she grabs the railing to step down onto the first metal rung. The metal is so cold and rusty that it's painful to touch. She pulls her hand back but knows she only has a few moments before the guys outside the door will be inside the apartment. So she pulls the collar of her coat up to cover her cheeks and steps down the ladder onto the second story fire escape. She begins to move even quicker when the light flicks on in their apartment. She finally reaches the bottom rung stepping down into the soft snow. Xavier grabs her by the arm startling her.

"Holy shit you scared me!" Nina exclaims.

"Come on…let's go before they realize we're out here!" Xavier continues to pull her. They head away from the building, taking off into the Moscow night. They walk for what seems to be hours ending up on a quiet residential block. Xavier continues to look around squinting under the dim street lights. He realizes that Nina has slowed down drastically; she is no longer at his side but has fallen way behind.

Nina is exhausted. Her feet are cold and numb. She doesn't know where Xavier is going. Her thoughts drift to a month ago when she took Benjamin's life. She misses him from time to time. He was so sincere, so uncomplicated, but an unnecessary obstacle. She can still feel the vibration of the gun in her hand as she pulled the trigger. The heat…she can feel the heat of Xavier grabbing her by the hand pulling her out of her thoughts. They finally reach a house and walk up to the door.

"Where are we Zay?" Nina asks shivering.

"An old business acquaintance. I just hope he's here," Xavier responds praying that his friend opens the door. Xavier continues to look around hoping that Gabriel's goons weren't following them. He rings the doorbell a few more times and knocks on the door vigorously. Finally, a light from behind the door comes on. A short bald man in a white T-shirt and pin-striped boxers swings the door open. He stands there looking at the worn out, nearly frozen couple.

"Do you have any idea what time it is?" His voice is deep and raspy but he doesn't bare the same accent as everyone else they've encountered in Moscow. He's American. He looks them up and down.

"Sam, it's me. Xavier. Please we just need somewhere to stay for a few hours so we can warm up. I promise we just need a few hours of sleep and a warm blanket. Whatever you can do we'd greatly appreciate it." Xavier hones in his power of persuasion with every word staring his old "friend" in the eyes.

The old man finally gives in, "I know who you are damn it! Just come in." He steps aside letting them walk into his home. He walks down the long narrow hallway showing them to a bedroom. "You can stay in the guest room. Twist the handle by the fireplace to turn on the heat. Bathroom is across the hall. Linens are in that closet. I don't want to know what you've gotten yourself into this time Xavier but I don't have enough money here for your kind of problems. You have to be out of here before I get home from work tomorrow." The grumpy old man retreats to his bedroom closing his door behind him before Xavier can thank him for his hospitality.

The guest room is fairly large with a large mahogany desk in the corner. Nina looks at Xavier who's already turned on the fire and is kneeling down in front of the flames trying to warm his hands. As the blood begins to warm and circulate throughout her body, Nina feels like pins and needles are under her skin. They undress hanging their clothes over a chair near the fireplace.

"So it seems Sam already knows what kind of trouble we're in. What happened before?" Nina asks as they begin to settle in for the night.

"Nina I really don't want to talk about it. All I'm going to say is I was in a bind a few years ago while I was over here and he helped me. Even though it took me a rather long time to repay him, I finally did. Either way, we can stay here until we figure out how we're going to get Gabriel his money."

"I can figure that out. Does that computer work?" she asks him motioning over toward the laptop sitting on the desk.

"I don't see why it shouldn't," Xavier shrugs. He turns his attention back to the fire. Nina wraps herself in the blanket that was draped across the king-size bed and walks over to the desk. She sits down in the plush leather chair and pushes the power button. The laptop powers on and luckily enough it has a guest option. She logs on and immediately goes online to instant message her old roommate Jeremy, who's back in the U.S:

Hey it's Eva…Just wanted to know if the salon was full? Can you fit me in?

Translation: Hey, it's Nina. Wanted to know if the cops are still searching for me heavy? Can I come back into the States?

She waits for a response unsure of what time it was in New York. His icon lights up a few minutes later showing him to be online.

Jeremy writes back:

Hey Eva. Long time no speak. Hope your hair is holding up but the chair is empty. Make sure you don't tamper with it. Are you coming in soon?

Translation: Hey Nina. Long time no speak. Hope everything is going okay but the coast is clear. You should change your look to be safe. When are you coming?

She replies to him:

Probably not, I'm enjoying the sunny skies and tropical breezes. I won't change a thing but I'll be there in a few weeks, I need a trim. Until the last time.

Translation: I have to come back, the weather is freezing. I'll figure something out but I'll be there in a few days, I need some money. Talk to you later.

Jeremy answers:

Okay. Until the last time.

Translation: Okay talk to you later.

They both log off their computers.

Jeremy sits back in his chair just staring at his computer screen. He knows that Nina's on the run with Xavier. Right after the blood bath at La Rouge, Nina began messaging him under the alias Eva Sloane. She had him set up a safe deposit box at a small time local bank. All of her money, well Xavier's embezzled cash and liquidated assets, were sitting nicely inside the box. In return, for his help, she lets him dip in the stash whenever he needs to. While she doesn't completely trust him, she knows that he is fully aware of what she will do to him if he ever gets too greedy.

Jeremy doesn't know whether he should be happy she's coming

home or worried that she might get arrested when she sets foot onto U.S. soil. He checks the time, it's a little past eight which means she's in some sort of trouble contacting him at four in the morning, Moscow time. He can only imagine what will happen when she arrives.

Nina can only imagine what may happen when she steps off of a plane in the U.S. She gets out of the chair after shutting down the laptop. She tells Xavier that Jeremy is expecting her and she has to change her look. She goes into the bathroom and begins to search through the cupboards and medicine cabinet. Her search yields a drug store box of dye, a bottle of peroxide and a finely-engraved silver straight razor. She pulls her mousy brown hair back into a pony tail, takes the razor, and with one swift motion cuts her hair off. The strands fall effortlessly to the floor. Seeing the hair fall feels like a new start for Nina. She pulls the band off her hair letting it fall. The new cut is short in the back and falls a bit longer in the front, framing her face rather nicely. She mixes the contents of the box dye with some peroxide to continue her transformation. By the time she's finished dying her hair and showering she's a brand new strawberry blonde. The change is so shocking she has to look at her reflection twice. She cleans up the bathroom making sure to clean up her excess hairs in a tissue to throw into the fire. She wraps her damp hair in a towel, and shuts out the light.

Xavier is on the computer when she enters the room. He doesn't look up from what he's doing but speaks to her chuckling, "I was wondering if you had drowned in there or something."

"No, just a quick change up," she responds taking the towel off her head, and drops it by the door. He turns, looking at her briefly. He does a double take and then gets up from the desk.

He walks toward her, circling her, taking in her new appearance. "What did you do?" He runs his fingers through what is left of her hair.

"You don't like it?" Her eyes shift down to the floor as she suddenly begins to doubt the extremeness of her change.

"It's not that I don't like it...It's just different...Really different," his blue eyes burrowed deep into hers. He felt a yearning for her. A feeling he hasn't felt in a while.

The mood struck him out of nowhere. He can't resist her, their lips meet and tongues intertwine. The tiny hairs along Nina's arms rise as the passion between them builds. Xavier's arm wraps around her waist; resting his palm on the small of her back. He pulls her in close. Her nipples are hard. He can feel them through her T-shirt pressing up against his warm body. He runs his hands over them. Nina can feel her pleasure moistening. She breathes heavily waiting for Xavier to take her.

The animal raging inside of him is aching to break free. He turns her around to face the bed, cupping her ass cheeks with both of his hands.

He grabs them hard lifting and spreading them slightly. He nearly lifts her off her feet causing her to fall forward bracing herself against the bed. He leans forward grabbing her hair and yanks her head back. She grunts trying to keep quiet. There is a moment when she thinks the old man is listening outside the door. Xavier rubs his stubbly beard against the side of her face then kisses on her neck. His teeth barely graze her skin sending chills up and down her body. He moves his hand under the shirt and between her legs to feel her. Nina is warm and wet.

"Get on the bed," he commands. "On your knees."

Nina obeys without uttering a sound. She waits there on her hands and knees waiting for his manhood to enter her. But instead she feels the soft touch of his tongue between her lips. His hands are grasping her thighs as they begin to tremble. He tastes her juices as they drip out from her walls. He curls his tongue around her clitoris. He sucks it gently moving his mouth from the top of her vagina to the bottom. He had always enjoyed the flavor of her womanhood. He strokes himself as he licks her as if he can't get enough. He teases her, sticking his tongue inside of her. He finally pulls his face from between her lips, stands up and plunges himself deep inside of her.

Doggie style is one of Nina's favorite positions as she grasps the covers with every pump. He is average length and a little skinny, but luckily for her his tongue more than makes up for the mediocre equipment. Xavier continues to pound into her until he finally succumbs to the wetness of her pleasure. He releases his orgasm with a few quick stutter pumps and a long sigh of relief. Nina asks him to give her the towel she dropped by the door. He hands it to her and then collapses next to her on the bed. She wipes them both clean. Without another word spoken, they soon fall asleep.

The aroma of coffee swirls in Nina's nostrils as she stirs under the warm blanket. The sun is barely peeking in through the drapes when she turns over to see Xavier is not in the bed next to her. She sits up in the bed and runs her fingers through her short hair. The feeling causes memories of the previous night to flood her thoughts suddenly making her afraid. What happened to the goons that were chasing them? Surely they know they climbed out of the window by now. Of course they tracked their footprints in the snow. But why weren't they being gagged and carried away? Why haven't they been found?

Xavier comes into the bedroom with a fresh plate of eggs, sausage and toast interrupting the twenty-one questions buzzing through Nina's head. He sets the plate down on the nightstand next to her, leaves and comes back into the room with coffee for the two of them. Nina dives into the food as if she had never eaten before. Xavier laughs at the ferocity at which she attacks her food. She moans and even grunts at one point.

"I guess someone was hungry," he retorts when she finally stops to take a breath.

She giggles. "Yes, I was starving! We were supposed to go out to eat last night, but you didn't come back when you said you were. I went to bed. You woke me up. We slushed through the snow. Now we're here. And now I'm eating."

"So is this all you need to lift your spirits? A good plate of food and a haircut?"

She stops eating and runs her fingers through her short hair again. She turns to look at him and her playful grin is no longer present. Worry and anxiety replace the meaningless joy that was just beaming from her eyes. "Xavier they're going to kill you when they find us, and I have no idea what they're going to do with me."

"We got here safe and sound. I made us walk in so many circles last night they don't know which way we went. They're not tracking us. Nobody is going to die. Don't worry so much. Just eat and let me worry about them and getting you out of here so nobody *has* to die." He reaches over and rubs the top of her hair like a puppy. She hates it when he does that. Xavier always knows how to minimize the intensity of any situation that they get into.

Nina doesn't speak anymore, but finishes her breakfast. Xavier takes her plate once she's done and leaves the room. He tells her to get herself together so they can leave. She spends the rest of the morning wiping down the room, the bathroom and the kitchen. She grabs the trash from the bathroom, pulls the sheets and blankets off the bed and carries them outside to an old metal barrel in the backyard. She tosses everything inside and sets it ablaze. The amber flames dance as the smoke billows up into the crisp morning air. It's below freezing outside but she can't feel it as much in her oversized sweatshirt and jeans. All she can feel is the warmth of the fire. She kicks her feet through the snow for a while until she finds a stick to poke the fire with. She stirs the contents in the fire making sure the dampness in the air doesn't put it out.

Nina finally decides to go back inside. Xavier hadn't given his typical, "We gotta go…hurry the fuck up!" in a while. When she walks into the bedroom she sees why. The man sitting in the chair at the desk isn't Xavier, and it isn't the grumpy old man who let them in last night. She wants to take a few steps backward out of the room before the stranger notices her, but the hammer cocking back on the gun burying into her head stops her dead in her tracks. The barrel of the gun digs into her scalp nudging her forward into the bedroom. Xavier is nowhere to be found.

The man in the chair turns around as they both walk into the room. The man behind the gun speaks, "Where is he?"

"Where is who?" she asks playing dumb. Her playfulness gets her struck across the face with the gun. Nina cries out in pain falling onto the bed. Her ear is ringing as she scrunches up her face in pain.

The man in the chair leans back with his hands folded, "I wouldn't play dumb Eva. My friend there doesn't appreciate when people waste his time." Nina looks up from the bed still clutching the side of her face. "My companion is going to speak to you again." The man in the chair nods his head to the man with the gun.

"Where is Jared?" he asks Nina, but this time he's standing in front of her looking down with the gun staring her in the face.

Nina becomes flustered and her face turns beet red. She forces tears to stream from her eyes, "I-I-I-don't know where Jay is. He was just here cooking me breakfast and I swear I don't know where he is or where he went but but bu- bu- bu-but I was in the backyard. I-I-I-I-I." She manages to work herself up into a fully blubbering female in distress.

"Hmm. Seems like Jared left you here for us. Sevastian, grab her and let's go."

The man with the gun, Sevastian, holsters his weapon and without a second to think about it hoists Nina up and over his shoulder.

"Oh my God! What are you doing? What are you going to do with me? Where are we going? HEEEEEEEELLLLLPPPP! SOMEBODY

PLEEEEEEEEEAAASSSE! HELP MEEEEEEEEEEE!!!!" Nina screams at the top of her lungs kicking and beating his back with her fists, trying to get the strange man to put her down. The man in the chair gets up and walks over to Nina who stops screaming when she sees him approaching. She is red in the face, with tears flowing down her cheeks, and blood rushing to her head as she hangs over Sevastian's shoulder.

The man in the chair grabs both her wrists in one of his hands and her chin with the other, "We aren't going to hurt you unless you waste our time. You, my dear, are going to see Gabriel. He will decide what is to be done with you. But until then, sleep." He pricks her in the neck with some type of needle and she is out cold almost instantaneously.

Chapter 3

"Strayer! In here now!" The commander of their unit sounds irritated as Ana and Greg walk down the hall into his office. Both of them appear timid and uncertain as to what they did to anger their boss. "I didn't ask for you Greg but you can stay since I'm pretty sure you know what's going on with Ana and her sister anyway." Greg nods and takes a seat next to Ana.

"I just got off the phone with an officer who busted your sister Anastasia for possession and intent to distribute. Apparently she pulled your card and told them she's working for us as a CI. Now you know as well as I do that is not what we do here. They're holding her until you get there as a courtesy! BUT...she's not getting off!"

"But sir—" Ana speaks up trying to offer an excuse.

"NO! She's getting booked and what the hell is going on with this Nina Slade? Do we have a lead as to where we can find her?" The commander looks at Greg.

"We need to speak to the security guard who was on duty the night of the incident, but he's already in lockup. We can't get to him without his lawyer being present, and his lawyer can't be found. So we're looking at other sources," Greg answers.

"I'll call in a favor so you two can get in to talk to him since he has information that can help us bring her in. Strayer...I don't know how deep your sister is in, but whatever it is, just remember you have a job to do! Now get out of my office."

"Yes sir," Ana and Greg say simultaneously getting up out of their chairs to leave. They go back to work sorting through the paperwork that Detective Flynn gave them. Ana can barely concentrate as thoughts of her sister surge through her mind. Finally slamming her hands on the papers in front of her, she gives up on work and storms out of the office. Greg feels like he should follow her but knows that at least one of them has to be focused on the task at hand. It had only been three days since Anna Lee asked her to find their sister. *Whelp*, she's been found.

Ana is pacing in the staircase trying to figure out exactly how she can help Asia, especially if the cops who grabbed her are as adamant as her boss is about her being booked. She knows she can't let that informant story fly, it'll reflect badly on her entire unit. Ana finally summons the courage to call the arresting officer and speak to him. She wants to persuade them in some way to get her sister off with a warning, maybe some kind of community service.

She speaks with the officer for a while getting the gist of the situation and what she can do to help. Then she begins to wonder what she's going to tell her sissy, Anna Lee. Lee is going to be so upset when she finds out there isn't really anything she can do for their sister, even as a Marshal.

Greg comes into the staircase looking for Ana and finds her just as she's getting off of the phone. Ana's face is riddled with exhaustion. Greg steps right in front of her; he looks her in the eye and moves the curly red tendril out of her face. He embraces her and she exhales into his chest. After a brief moment of peace he grasps her by the shoulders and moves her back staring her in the face again saying, "Okay slut are you ready to get back to fucking work now?"

The vulgarity is just what she needs to change her mindset so she can get her head back into the hunt for Nina. She responds to him, "Yeah asshole, I'm ready. What's up?"

"Boss man got us ten minutes with the security guard but we have to go now."

Ana and Greg leave the staircase behind along with Ana's emotions. They get down to the county jail in no time and are soon face to face with the man who should have seen it all.

After talking with the security guard for their ten minutes, all they know is that he was paid five thousand up front to turn the cameras off and another five thousand when Nina left the building. He told them that when Nina and Blake showed up, Blake was a bit disheveled but didn't say anything to let him know she was in any kind of trouble. He heard different stories and rumors about Blake's sexual escapades and figured it was one of her kinky moments. He thought they were going to have sex in Blake's glass encased office. He had no idea what was going on upstairs, nor did he care at the time. He never saw Ivan and David enter the building because he purposely found something else to do other than look at the cameras. He knew if he really wanted to see what was going on up there his buddy in the IT department could get him a copy of the tape. He never thought that people were being shot and killed. He would have never taken the money if that was the case. Greg and Ana had asked him about the money and if he would turn it over. The security guard conveniently spent it all before his arrest. They thanked him for his time and left the facility.

Driving back to the office almost seems pointless for Ana. She looks at Greg who is watching the scenery pass by from the passenger seat. She wants to go straight to the precinct where her sister is being held to try and negotiate her release. She knows that Greg wouldn't mind, but this is her first job back in the field and doesn't want to jeopardize it by allowing her family to disrupt their investigation.

Greg interrupts her thoughts, "Ana, let's go get her."

"What are you talking about Greg?"

"Asia… I know you're worried about her and it won't help either one of us if you're distracted. We're already out here; let's just go check on her, find out what we can do, if anything, and get back to work."

Ana smiles on the inside; relieved that Greg is so understanding of what she's going through. Greg knows that in order for Ana to function as the great officer she is, she needs to know her sisters are okay. Not to mention that he wants to get promoted and bringing in Nina Slade will be the boost his resume needs.

He looks over at Ana wondering when will be the right time to tell her he's looking for a promotion. She won't be happy about getting a new partner. Some day he will, someday soon, but not today.

They arrive at the precinct where Anastasia is being held. Ana walks inside while Greg waits inside the car. Ana immediately flashes her credentials and is brought to the room where Asia is sitting chained to a table. The room is gray with no windows. There isn't a two way mirror. There aren't any officers on the other side of the wall listening in. It's just her sister, sitting in there alone. She is disheveled and alone. She is dirty and alone. She needs a shower and a warm bed, but here she sits... alone. Ana looks at her sister. She is frail and looks hungry. She takes the chair and moves it next to her. She sits down and takes Asia's hands into hers. Asia looks at Ana. Her green eyes are so dark, bloodshot, as she is coming down off her most recent high. Her beautiful brown hair is matted and dirty.

"Sissy," Ana whispers to Anastasia trying very hard not to cry for her.

"Belle," Asia smiles at her. She is barely coherent. She inhales deeply as the tears begin to roll down her cheeks, "Belle...Sissy...I messed up. I messed up big."

"It's okay Sissy," Ana runs her hand over her sister's hair, "It's okay, I'm here, I'm going to help you. You gotta tell me what happened. What happened Sissy?"

"If I tell you, you can't tell Lee. She's gonna be so mad at me. Do you promise?"

"Yes Sissy I promise."

"I went to my happy place you know," Asia starts to explain but she's getting frantic and anxious with every word, "And a-an-a-an- and when I got there Danny was there, not Tuto. Danny, you know, Danny was there not Tuto. And a-an- -an- and I wanted my usual, you know, so-so I asked him for my usual you know. Bu-bu-but I didn't have any money you know cuz I never have the money cuz-cuz Tuto, Tuto is usually there you know, not Danny. Bu-bu-but Danny said Tuto ain't comin back you know so I asked him should I just blow him like I do Tuto, and he gets upset a-an-a-an-and hits me in the face. And a-an-a-an-and I don't know what he wants so-so-so I ask him what does he want so I can get to my happy place a-an-a-an- and he says, 'HERE TAKE THIS', and a-an-a-an-and he shoves this package in my face with a note a-an-a-an- and says go to that address leave the package and come back to him so so so I can get my usual you know."

At this point, Asia breaks down and starts crying. "I didn't wanna do it Sissy, but you gotta do what Danny says or he kills you. HE KILLS YOU SISSY! So I didn't wanna do it but I did, a-an-a-an- and I didn't wanna do it but went," Asia keeps muttering the last sentence over and over again.

Anabelle looks at her sister, and she is filled with so much pain that she couldn't have helped her before they got to this point. She runs her hand over her hair and kisses her sister on the forehead. She wishes she would have paid her more attention when the drug abuse first started. This would have never happened.

She takes Asia's face in her hands and wipes away her tears with her thumbs. Ana looks her in the eye, "Sissy I know you didn't wanna do anything, but you gotta tell me what happened so I can help you.”

“I can fill you in on the rest since you didn’t want to hear it over the phone,” the arresting officer comes inside the room interrupting them. “Your sister brought a kilo of cocaine to one of our undercovers.”

“*A whole brick?* Get the fuck outta here! No way,” Ana denies the accusation.

The officer cocks his head to the side, shocked at her vulgar demeanor, “Uh yes way. She had it in her hand...was gonna drop it and run but the officer convinced her to come inside to try the product and that’s where I come in. This is the fourth time within the last three months we’ve busted your sister, Strayer. AND EVERY TIME! You come in here on your white stallion to save the day. But not today Marshal! Just like I said earlier! Not today!” He slams his hand on the desk shaking Asia’s chains, waking her from the lull she was in.

“How can you seriously do your job upholding the law, bringing in criminals, but when it’s your sister all of a sudden the goddamn law doesn’t apply?!”

“I don’t know who you think you’re talking to officer, but you’re beneath the pay grade of your tone,” Ana imposes her authority as she stands from the table looking the officer square in his eyes. Her blue eyes are shocking and strong, almost making him back down.

The officer, however, stands his ground, "I don't know who you think you're talking to but this arrest doesn't concern your pay grade! So if you're not the member of the bar association who is representing Anastasia Strayer then your time is up and your favors are officially cashed out!" The officer is firm with his statement moving toward the door and motioning for Anabelle to leave. Ana looks at the officer and then at the open door. She shakes her head, not willing to go to war with this officer, especially since he's right. She touches her sister's hand one last time before telling her she's going to figure a way to get her out of this. Ana storms out of the room without another word to the officer. She doesn't know what she's going to do, and worst of all she has to be the one to tell Lee what's going on. Lee is going to be disappointed in the both of them. Asia for getting herself into another situation, and Ana for not being able to prevent it. Ana is feeling furious, confused, worried, anxious and helpless as she marches out of the police station.

Greg looks at a very pissed off Ana storming his way. "I'm guessing Asia won't be getting out any time soon?" he asks as she opens the door to get into the car.

"They booked her on a brick of coke with intent to distribute. She was trying to get high and the dealer she normally deals with wasn't there. So the new guy, I guess the old dealer's partner or whatever sends her on a dummy run so she got busted with it instead of him."

"Well she can make a deal to set him up right? Isn't that how these narcotics cases work?"

"I don't know Greg," she snaps turning the car on, "The cop in there is a fucking douchebag on his almighty fucking high horse and I'm outta of fuckin favors and goddamn it my sister's a fuckin' junkie! God… Fucking…Damn… It!" Ana beats the steering wheel with her fists. Banging her hands in frustration shakes the car and the bun loose atop her head allowing the tight red curls to fall. Her face is almost as red as her hair. She looks to Greg, with no idea as to what she needs from him right now.

Greg rarely catches Ana in this state of vulnerability. He can't stand to see her this way but has no idea how to help her. He looks into her big blue eyes, big blue eyes that are seconds away from shedding tears, and plays the role he plays best; her partner.

"Ana listen to me. You cannot and will not always be able to save your sister. I've watched you LITERALLY pull her out of the gutter and try time and time again to clean her up. Eventually, you have to stop babying her and let her accept responsibility for her own life. It's HER life not yours! You are not above the law and she has to answer for whatever she has done. Now, I'm not telling you to stop being her sister but at this point there is NOTHING that you can do to get her out of this. Now stop being such a pussy, pull your fucking panties up and let's get back to fucking work!"

Ana rubs the tears from her eyes, wipes her nose on her sleeve, and focuses on the road pulling away from the precinct and her sister. She thanks Greg for his words; the verbal kick in the ass to get back to the task at hand. They need to track down Nina and as of right now they are dead in the water. They decide to grab a bite to eat at a nearby restaurant. They sit down for lunch and only talk about the case; recapping on what Blake and the security guard told them. Greg takes out his notes and continually looks over them as he eats his lunch. Finally he sees something they missed.

"Hey Ana, did you happen to go over any notes from Flynn about this Jeremy guy?"

"Uhh, I think I read over his name but it wasn't much to go on. The Benjamin guy told Flynn that Jeremy didn't know where Nina was. When Flynn spoke to him he said the same thing. He didn't know where she was and she didn't leave any forwarding address."

"Hmmm, don't you find it odd that a girl with a roommate who she's lived with for years just disappears and the roommate has no idea where she went?"

"I guess. What's on your mind?"

"Well maybe we should pay him a visit and talk to him. Maybe you can strong arm him a bit into remembering something he forgot to tell Flynn."

Ana chuckles at his suggestion, "How about we just get a warrant to tap his phones and computer? He's not going to tell us anything if he truly doesn't know where she is. But I tell you what, if they are as close as you think they are then she's going to reach out to him eventually. Even if it's just to say, 'Hey, I'm okay.'"

Greg nods in agreement with her suggestion and starts making calls to get the taps set up as soon as possible. He excuses himself from the table so he can go outside to finish his calls. While sitting at the table, it's hard for Ana not to think about her sister sitting there in the precinct. All of the emotions begin to surge again. She buries her face in her hands to stop the impending wave of anxiety.

"You look like you can use something a bit stronger than that soda," a man's voice speaks to her.

Ana picks her head up to see Wren standing there at her table. She smiles and for a brief moment forgets about her sisters. He looks good in the daylight, even sexier when she's sober. His chiseled body shows through everything he wears. His goatee is trimmed short; his black hair cut real low, his essence is so domineering it commands attention. He asks her if he can sit; a gesture that she kindly obliges.

She asks him about his day and how he ended up here at her table. He gives her the short version that he had something to do for work and decided to grab a bite to eat when he saw the mop of red curls spilling onto the table. She laughs as she runs her fingers through her hair, all the while smirking at her trademark. He offers to buy her lunch but she lets him know that she's eaten already.

"You know, you look amazing when you're sober Anabelle," he says to her.

"You know I was just thinking the same thing about you," she smiles. "You also look amazing when I'm sober."

He snickers at her quip, "You know I don't think I've had you sober since that first week we started messing around."

"That's a lie," she laughs. She pauses to stop and actually think about the last time she's had sex without being drunk and disorderly.

"That look of bewilderment on your face says I'm not lying," he laughs at her expression. But suddenly his expression changes from lighthearted to mischievous. He moves his hand under the table and rubs her inner thigh. The touch is so subtle but instantly makes Ana moist. She wants him to fuck her on the table, right there in the middle of the restaurant. Now all she can imagine is the other morning, and his manhood standing at full attention. She wasted a good erection that morning because she wasn't sober enough to realize who she was sleeping with. As good as he looks to her right now, her body craves him. She yearns for him to touch her, to kiss her, to slide inside of her. She wants to feel the intensity of his full girth making her climax, dripping down all over him. Wren has moved his hand from the inside of her thigh to the inside of her jeans. He was very discreetly rubbing her clitoris with one hand and leaning on the table with his other. He is positioned in such a way that he seems to be having a normal conversation with her, but her facial expressions are a dead giveaway. She can barely control her urges to moan in ecstasy. Just before the waitress comes over with the check, he pulls his hands out of her pants and folds them neatly in front of him on the table.

"Can I get you two any dessert?" the waitress asks completely unaware of what was just happening.

"No thank you ma'am, I've had my dessert already," Wren answers without missing a beat. He licks his fingers as if he had just finished scooping some icing off of a fresh piece of cake.

"No thank you," Ana shakes her head barely able to utter her refusal for anything else. The waitress walks away shaking her head. Once she's far enough away, Ana slaps Wren in the shoulder.

"Hey what the hell was that for?" he asks playing along as if it hurt.

"What the hell?! I'm on duty! You just can't follow me into a restaurant and play with my pussy under the table like it's okay!" She tries to keep her voice just below a whisper.

"You like it when I play with it," he says with a smile.

"Shut up! You're distracting me!"

"You needed a distraction the way you were looking when I walked up to you. Looks like you've been having a pretty rough day. You want to tell me about it?"

"Not right now. Maybe we can go grab a drink or something after physical therapy later."

"You know just because that's been the way we've been meeting up these past few months, doesn't mean that has to be the only way. I'll come to you even when you're not drunk," he says with a smirk.

"I'm sure you will...Pervert!" They both laugh at her dirty mind.

"Ana, seriously," he rubs her hand lightly, "We can go grab something to eat and a nonalcoholic beverage after therapy and we can talk about your rough day or not talk about it. Okay?"

"Okay," Ana agrees to his proposal, "A sober date with my designated dick. Oops did I say that out loud? I meant my designated driver."

Wren shakes his head at her as he stands from the table. He leans down and kisses her on the cheek before saying goodbye and walking away.

Ana is completely smitten with him but now it seems like things are about to get complicated. He wants to deal with her sober. She isn't completely comfortable with that; although she's sure he's tired of having her pull her gun out every time she's too drunk to remember who brought her home the night before. Yet, there's something about him that makes him seem like a good idea. She's in thoughts and daydreams about her lover when Greg finally returns to the table.

"Hey was that Wren I just saw leaving here?"

"Yeah, just a coincidence," she tells Greg with a smirk. He doesn't know why she's smiling, but is glad that she is. Her emotional side is just too much for him to comprehend, and way more than what he's willing to deal with.

"Well next time you see him tell him I said thank you. Whatever he said to you definitely took you out of that dark place you were in. Tell him to teach me his secret so I know how to pull you out next time."

Ana laughs, "Believe me, what he did to change my mood, you don't want to do and your wife DEFINITELY doesn't want you to do."

"Alrighty then," Greg scrunches up his face at the thought of what could have possibly happened at the table while he was outside on the phone. "Well I got what we needed to listen into this Jeremy guy's phones. I'm gonna have the tech guys set up a live stream on our server so we can listen into everything. And hopefully he can give us some info about where we can find Nina Slade."

Chapter 4

Nina barely opens her eyes, and for a split second the woman leaning over her looks like Blake forcing her to react, "No! No! No! How did you find me? Bitch! Leave me alone! I Should Have Killed You Too! I Should Have Killed You!"

Her hallucinogenic state subsides when the woman says, "*Devushka,* calm down...calm down." The woman strokes Nina's hair like a toddler she's trying to soothe back to sleep.

Nina looks at the woman, sitting up trying to get her bearings. She's sitting in a bed a bit smaller than a twin size. Looks like one of those roll away beds she used to see on those late night TV Land sitcoms; I Love Lucy and such. The sheets look dirty but stink of fresh bleach. The room is cold and dark. The dark wooden floors and chipped gray walls do nothing to spread light throughout the space. The room is spinning, the knot in her stomach is rising, and her gag reflex is trying its hardest to keep the contents of her gut where they are. She gags again and starts to look around. The woman grabs the trash can by the bed just in time for Nina to lose her battle with her gag reflex, emptying her stomach into the garbage. The woman holds her hair out of her face while she hurls into the can. Once Nina stops, the woman brings her some straight vodka in a glass. Nina, believing it's water, takes it straight back but immediately spits it out into the trash can. The alcohol burns her lips and the back of her throat.

"Uh what the fuck was that?" she asks the woman while clearing her throat and wiping her mouth with the back of her hand.

"It was vodka, it helps with the nausea," she speaks to Nina through a thick Russian accent.

"Where am I?" Nina asks still looking around. She doesn't remember what happened after the man scooped her up in the house where Xavier left her alone for the goons. He must have saw them coming and decided to leave. She can't believe he left her there like that. He knows what kind of men these are and he left her there. *Fucking coward.*

"You, my dear, are in Gabriel's Garden."

"Where?" Nina asks more confused.

"The men who bring you here, they bring all the good girls here. You make good money, pay your debt in few years," the woman tries to explain but Nina doesn't understand what's going on.

"I don't owe a debt! My husband is the one who owes the debt! The two men, who are after him, grabbed me."

"*Devushka*, it's okay. You, your husband, not matter to Gabriel as long as he gets his money."

"*De- de- devushka*? Why do you keep calling me that?"

"Oh I sorry, it mean girl in Russian, I do not know your name."

"It's Ni- it's Eva, Eva Sloane," Nina answers her, almost forgetting her alias. "But what do you mean, umm, pay your debt in few years? How am I supposed to do that?"

"Sweet Eva, you are in Gabriel's Garden."

"Yeah you said that before!" Nina is beginning to get frustrated, even though the woman is trying hard to make her very comfortable. "I need to get out of here. How do I get out of here?"

The woman giggles, "No girl leave here unless with Sevastian."

Nina remembers his name, the big dude who slapped her with the gun and threw her over his shoulder right before she passed out. She has no idea how long she was even unconscious. Then she wakes up in this dark place because that coward left her. She swings her feet down to the floor finally noticing the cold metal shackle clamped around her ankle. She is chained to the bed. The bed is bolted to the floor. Her clothes are also gone. She has been lying there in nothing but her bra and panties. She reaches down for the shackle running her fingers over the aged metal. It's rough and cold to the touch. It scrapes the skin around her ankle if she moves around too much. She pulls at the linked chain attached to it; not even sure what it's anchored to, but knows she's not going anywhere.

"I have to use the bathroom," Nina tells the woman.

"Here…use this," she says passing her the bucket she just puked in. Nina decides to postpone urinating. She'd rather pee all over herself before peeing in that bucket. She shakes her head wondering how the hell she's going to get out of this.

"When do I speak to Gabriel?"

"Soon, soon, he tells you how long you work here, and then you be prettiest new flower in Gabriel's Garden? Yes? Yes…you be prettiest new flower," the woman says sounding like she is trying to convince herself of that last statement.

"YOU KEEP FUCKING SAYING THAT!!! WHAT THE FUCK IS GABRIEL'S

GARDEN?!" Nina snaps angrily at the woman.

"It's okay Lana, that will be all," a man says from the doorway. The woman who had been talking to and caring for Nina gets up from her seat and leaves the room.

The man stands at a staggering six feet two inches. His hair looks soft, full, but its whitish gray color reveals his age a bit. His white beard connects with his moustache and comes down a few inches below his chin. His eyes are dark brown but you can tell by looking into his face and at his skin that he's lived a very hard life. The scar that runs from the top of his left eyebrow straight down to his chin is proof of that. It even runs through his facial hair marking a trail like a river on a map.

He walks toward Nina and takes a seat in the same chair the woman was just sitting in. Nina isn't exactly sure but this man makes her very afraid. His calmness is doing nothing to hide the true beast of his character. His essence, his very being, embodies a force she can't ignore. She looks down at his hands. They are calloused and rough. She pulls her feet back onto the bed and the sheet over her legs up to her waist. She folds her hands in her lap and looks at them refusing to make eye contact with the man.

"What you are feeling right now is normal Eva. People have two distinct reactions when they are in my presence. They either respect me or they fear me. And for what you have been through to get to this point, it is understandable that you fear me. I am Gabriel. And welcome to my garden," his voice is monotone, no inflection, no reasonable reveal about the kind of mood he's in. His Russian accent is present but barely. She is sure that he can change the dialects with his voice to adjust to whatever country he's in. He's intelligent.

Nina rolls her eyes and shakes her head at the garden reference. Gabriel moves his hands from the arm rests to his lap, and the shift makes Nina flinch.

"You see Eva…Even though every fiber of your being is telling you to curse at me, to fight with me, to disrespect me as you just did; the slightest shift in my posture demands you not be so careless with your body language. I imagine it was that carelessness that got you that bruise on the side of your face."

Nina still refuses to make eye contact with him, and doesn't say a word. Even if she wanted to speak at this moment, words cannot describe the feeling she has sitting so close to a creature who is coldhearted and calculating.

"I will tell you Eva, that Gabriel's Garden is a place where my special friends come to pick my best flowers. All of the girls here, including you, are one of my precious flowers. The girls perform whatever activities imaginable by my friends and do not contest it! But you my dear are bruised and cannot be shown until that has healed. Sevastian will pay a part of your debt since he is responsible for you not being able to work right away. I run a very respectable exchange here. You will not be drugged, unless you prefer to be, and you will not be beaten unless you are wasting time. Time, my beautiful Daphne, is what I value most. More than money because you can NEVER get it back. You and your jackass husband wasted a lot of my time tracking you in circles through the snow when he should have never come to play without the money to pay me," he growls. Gabriel is more annoyed about the lack of principle in "Jared", but indeed grateful he left this beautiful flower for him.

"My name is Eva, and I had no idea what he was doing! This has nothing to do with me. Why do I have to pay for his debt?" Nina finally decides to speak hoping to get some answers.

Gabriel looks at her almost surprised that she mustered up the courage to say anything at all, "I only call you my Daphne because just like the flower you are beautiful but deadly. You must pay his debt because he was not there yesterday and you were. This morning I received a message from him saying that you are willing to do anything for him, and you will take care of it. Tell me how many people have you killed and how many have you killed for him?"

Nina is getting angrier and angrier by the moment refusing to answer his obscene question. The sheer cowardice of Xavier is unbelievable and she is more upset with herself that she has allowed him to use her over and over again to do his dirty work. She has had enough. The shackle around her ankle is irritating, this conversation is irritating, but she tries to keep calm and think of a way out of this room. She manages to subdue her rage and looks up into Gabriel's eyes.

"How much does Jay owe you Gabriel?"

Gabriel pulls out a small notebook from his pocket and flips through the pages. He uses his finger to scroll down the pages until he finally spots Jared Sloane. "Jared is in debt to me for fifty two thousand U.S. dollars."

"How can that be? He told me it was twenty the other night!"

"I don't know why he told you that but his balance is fifty two thousand. Now, I will deduct six hundred because of your face which brings the debt to fifty-one thousand four hundred. The girls make about twelve dollars an hour working a minimum of eight hours every day. Five of those dollars go toward your debt, three of those dollars go to a healthcare fund, three more dollars goes to room and board and I put the last dollar away for you until your debt is paid off. *IF* you make it… then you take what you have made and you get to leave. But honestly the only number you need to worry about is the five toward your debt. If you stay healthy and do what you are told and do not waste time you will be paid up in three years, five months and twenty three days. Okay...but for now, you rest and get well. I want to put you to work as soon as possible."

Nina can't believe Xavier has been involved with such a snake. She can't believe she followed him here to Russia. She can't believe she didn't see Xavier for who he really is. She looks at Gabriel sitting there, going over this plan, as if this sex trade is a legitimate employment opportunity for her with benefits.

"Gabriel, may I propose something to you? A better business deal of sorts?" Nina asks.

"Of course you may Eva. I'm always interested in making good deals," he says leaning forward fully interested in what she's about to say.

"By the time this bruise heals I can have twice the amount of money that is owed to you. I understand how much you value your time so I wouldn't dare waste it. I do not appreciate when people waste my time, which is why I am now infuriated with Jay. But if you let me go back to the States to get the cash, I can bring it back to you within a week or so. Let's eliminate the need to accumulate it over the next three years which we both know, I probably won't survive. I can give you one hundred four thousand and bring you Jared."

Gabriel sits back in his chair thinking about her proposal. She has a very good point. Her natural disobedience will make it very difficult for her to survive under these conditions and will make his special friends upset. She would be a continued disruption to business as usual and she will not last long enough to pay off the debt. Sevastian would kill her, and probably enjoy doing so.

Gabriel sets his terms of their agreement, "You make a very good proposition Eva. I like your practicality. However, instead of you paying me extra you will pay for travel fees. I will escort you to my private plane and fly you into the States. There you will be greeted by an escort, personally chosen by me. He will be by your side for the entire time you are there, and will accompany you back here. You pay me the fifty-one thousand, four hundred, and whatever the costs are for the plane and transportation of the escort. If you are lying to me, I will kill you. You have one week to go and come back with Jared and the money."

"Would you like him dead or alive?" she asks him unsure if he would add an additional challenge to her proposition.

"That, my beautiful Daphne is up to you," Gabriel answers her already knowing the decision she's going to make. He calls for Lana, the woman who was caring for Nina earlier. He tells her to bring her clothes and the key to release Nina from her shackle.

Nina is surprised that Gabriel listened to her and actually agreed to her proposal. Not only will she be able to travel back to the States in the luxury of a private jet, but the chances of her being flagged for stepping onto American soil is slim to none. Her only concern now is getting around the city when she gets back, and how the hell is she going to find Xavier?

Gabriel is sitting next to Nina in the back seat of his Cadillac Escalade, as his chauffeur drives them to a private landing strip somewhere outside of Moscow. A three person flight crew was getting ready for the flight. The car comes to a stop and Gabriel doesn't turn to look at her but maintains his position, staring through the front windshield. He speaks to her in a very calm tone, "Eva, I am giving you this opportunity because you are something special like me. You are not like my other flowers, my Daphne. You are something beautifully evil, and that husband of yours had no idea of what was in front of him or how to utilize you. I trust you will be back in the time I have allotted you. So there is no need for me to remind you of the consequences if you fail to produce what *you* proposed. My cousin, Sergio, will meet you on the American side. He will escort you where you need to go. And Eva?"

She turns to look at him, "Yes Gabriel?"

"The money alone is no good, Jared alone is no good. You either bring me both or I will take my time and skin you alive," he reminds her. Despite how nice and accommodating he has been with her he is still a beast that demands to be feared. Nina shivers at the thought of being filleted, but doesn't respond. There is no need for assurances from her at this moment. She knows what she needs to do and the sooner she gets it done, the sooner she can move on with her life.

She zips up the coat Gabriel gave her to wear and gets out of the car. She boards the plane and takes a seat. She looks around the aircraft. Seemingly Gabriel's Garden is doing very well. Although she is sure that is not his only means of income.

Nina takes the coat off and feels something in one of the pockets. She fishes through the heavy jacket and finds what the object is. It's a small cell phone. She powers it on. It has a full battery, there aren't any names or numbers stored in it, there aren't any messages or pictures to go through. There is only one number in the call history and she is almost positive that's the line to connect to Gabriel. She logs onto the internet and instantly goes to her messaging service.

She messages Xavier:

Jared, I know you're in a meeting but I've gone to get my hair cut. I should be done in about five hours. You know how long these appointments can take. Pick me up at the salon.

Translation: Xavier, I know you've made a run for it, but I've gone to get the money. I'll be back in five days. You know how these banks are. Meet me at the hotel by the airport.

She waits for a response, but nothing comes through. She wants to message Jeremy to let him know but something in her gut is telling her to see him in person. The ten hour flight is just what Nina needed to get some rest. She cherishes being able to sleep without the thought of someone chasing after her. She can't be caught if she's thousands of miles up in the air. The flight is as smooth as is its landing. She touches down in a small, private airport in Pennsylvania somewhere. She wakes up just in time for the captain to announce what the time and temperature is outside. She gathers her belongings and puts on the coat. The flight attendant opens the door and lowers the stairs.

Nina steps into the cold morning air, zipping her coat up before walking down the steps and onto the runway. She had only taken a few steps when a man approaches her from out of nowhere. She never saw which direction he came from. He is huge. He looms over her and his muscles are enormous. The dragon tattoo that wraps around his neck is clear as the sun is rising.

"You must be Sergio," Nina volunteers breaking the silence as they walk toward the tiny terminal.

"That is correct Eva," he replies to her.

"Well where are we going?" she asks him.

"We're going to my car so we can drive back up to New York."

Sergio seems distant to Nina. She figures this is only because if she fails at her task he has to deliver her to Gabriel. No sense in getting to know someone you might have to kill later. She shrugs her shoulders at the thought of why he doesn't seem too talkative. As they get into the car he insists that she drive; just follow the navigation until they get back to town. Nina is confused as to why he's making her drive. Yet, Sergio doesn't explain himself just tells her to get in and start the car.

She looks at him struggling to put his seat belt on. His muscle mass is so large he can barely turn to grab the buckle. Nina smirks at his bulk and suddenly imagines what he must look like naked. Shaking the thought loose from her head she leans over from the driver's seat and across his body to grab the seatbelt and click it in for him.

"Thank you," he says quietly.

"You smell good, what is that?" she asks trying to make small talk.

"Soap."

"Well what kind of soap?"

"Listen; let's not pretend like we need to get to know each other. You're here to do a job and I'm here to make sure it gets done. Kill the pleasantries and let's get this shit over with," he states allowing his irritation to show.

"I'm sorry this must be so inconvenient for you," Nina's sarcasm shines through every word.

"It is actually. I had to take a whole fucking week off work and for what? So you can go to the fucking bank!" he huffs to himself.

"Well my life is a tad bit important to me so I have to do this but no worries, I'll be out of your hair soon, and you can go back to work. I'm sure one of Gabriel's flowers needs you to tend to her," she smugly replies.

"I don't work for Gabriel! I don't tend to anything in that garden of his. I'm just doing this out of respect for him and all the things he's done for me. So just drive. Turn the GPS volume all the way up. The route back home is already plugged in, just press 'GO'! If I hear or see you rerouting or trying to deviate from our course I will end your life where you sit."

"Yeah right. You don't have a gun on you and you wouldn't attack me while I'm driving," Nina laughs at his threat. She can barely get her last chuckle out when his arm moves from his lap to her throat in lightning speed.

His fist is barely touching her throat but the pressure behind it is forcing her to gasp for air. She doesn't know what to do. She's craving oxygen so she forces a tear down her cheek. He moves his hand away from her. That first gasp of air is magical as she turns the key in the ignition. The engine roars muffling the sounds of her quiet whimpers.

"For the record never assume what anyone is carrying," he pulls out a gold plated, .44 caliber Desert Eagle hand cannon. He pulls the clip out and clicks it back into place. "Second, I don't need any manmade object to kill you. I train my body as my weapon; it is just as lethal as any bullet except I am more precise. Third, if I do that to you while you're driving; you'll be dead, the car will crash, and the air bags will deploy. Lastly, drive the fucking car!"

"Okay," she says quietly through her forced tears. Nina wants to extract some form of sympathy from him realizing if she can get him to soften up and eventually like her; he may be a valuable asset to her later.

"And cut the bullshit, I know the kind of person you have to be in order to strike a deal with Gabriel. Those tears ain't fooling me, so don't waste them here. You're a stone cold killer and I will not hesitate to put you down, just like you wouldn't hesitate in the moment if you needed to do me."

Nina stops crying immediately, smiling as she looks through the windshield out into the morning. "You are an impressive *being* Sergio. You're just as interesting as your cousin Gabriel. You two read people so well. I wish I had that talent."

"You don't need it. People like you and Gabriel don't need to read people, they read you and react accordingly."

"Hmmm, he said something similar about people in his presence. They either respect him or fear him. Do you fear me? Do you respect me? What do I evoke in you Sergio?"

"You evoke sleepiness. Now shut up and drive!" Sergio commands for the last time. Nina laughs at his sarcasm. She looks at him turning toward her, and closes his eyes. She wants to believe that he's asleep but knows he isn't. All she can do is stick to her plan to get the money, go back to Moscow and find Xavier. So without antagonizing him any further; she lets Sergio rest his eyes while she drives back to New York.

Chapter 5

The food sitting on their plates looks fresh out of a popular food magazine. It tastes just as good as it looks. Tommy Jay's is pretty full for a Thursday night dinner service, but Ana told Wren months ago that it's her favorite restaurant. So when he suggested they go out to eat and drink, *and not get drunk*, he remembered and made a reservation. The entire floor is buzzing and lively as Ana surveys the restaurant. She feels so guilty being out to eat when her sister, Asia, is still in lockup. She looks down at the food on her plate and continues to just pick at it. She shuffles her veggies around, and lightly taps the plate with her fork. Wren watches her playing with her food. He knows she was having a rough day when he saw her earlier around lunch, and physical therapy was no picnic today either.

"Do you want to talk about it?" he asks her.

"Yeah…sure…we can talk about how this food tastes different," she replies dodging the true answer to his question. She taps the arm of a waiter who happens to be passing by their table at the moment to ask him about the food. The waiter informs her that the food tastes a bit different because their head chef, Sergio, is out of town for the week. She thanks him for the information, and returns to shuffling the remainder of her food around her plate. Wren is beginning to think that a sober night between them may not have been the best idea for today.

"I thought the food was actually pretty good," Wren offers his opinion trying to develop an ongoing conversation.

"It is good," Ana says, "But it just tastes different. I can tell. This is my favorite meal from here, and no one makes my chicken stuffed with seafood as good as Sergio."

"I get it. I guess I'll just grab the check so we can go," he says as an offer to end this boring date. He makes a hand gesture to the waiter signaling him to bring over the tab. It arrives a few moments later; the waiter places it on the table offering them dessert, which they decline. Wren's thinking if he would have got her drunk they would be having sex in a bathroom right now. Yet, Wren knows that there's something special about Ana. He doesn't want to give up on her just yet. He knows that, whatever is bothering her, it's getting in the way of her enjoying herself right now. He decides to try one more time to get her to open up, "Is it work that's got you so down in the dumps?"

"No. I actually got cleared to be back in the field full time."

"So what is it? Is it me? Am I not interesting enough when you're sober?" he asks growing increasingly frustrated with the way the date is going.

Ana can sense his irritability, "Oh no Wren, it's not you. I got some issues going on with my sisters and there's nothing I can do to change or help the situation. I just feel like shit right now. My sister was locked up the other day and this is the last straw. Normally, I can pull a few strings to get her out of trouble. But this time, it was too much and too many times. I can't do anything. The officers working the case won't let me do anything, and even my commander is honoring their decision to not allow her any leeway because of her relation to me. I just feel so guilty being here. I can't enjoy myself knowing that she's in there. I'm sorry. I didn't mean to waste your time and money dragging me out tonight."

"No, don't apologize. I understand that family can often be a burden. You didn't waste my time or my money. I apologize for my frustration. Let's just get out of here. I'll take you home and we can try it again another night."

Ana agrees as Wren grabs her hand helping her get up from the table. He leaves some cash for the check and they walk out of the restaurant.

The drive to Ana's house is quiet for the most part. Sounds of light music playing through the car radio waft through the space. Ana's head is leaning against the window with a vacant stare painted across her face. Thoughts of her sister won't stop consuming her every waking moment. Wren looks over at her; she seems so distant. He touches her hand lightly which startles her out of her thoughts. She looks at him with a warm smile but still has nothing to say. She appreciates his effort to try and build something deeper between them but knows that her family and job will always get in the way of that. She never tries to develop any kind of real relationship with anyone specifically for these reasons. However, there's something inside of her saying that she shouldn't let Wren go. Right now all she wants to do is cuddle with him under her covers. She's okay with the silence between them.

They finally arrive at Ana's house where she invites Wren to come inside. He agrees, but with the mood she's been in he has no expectations.

They venture upstairs to her bedroom; a room that seems unbearably quiet when she's sober. She starts to take her clothes off. Her skin is smooth and soft, lightly tanned and sprinkled with freckles. He smiles watching her undress. She pulls the scrunchy out of her hair, unleashing those crimson curls from the messy bun. He loves running his fingers through her hair.

He approaches her taking his shirt off and tossing it onto a nearby chair. He looks deep into her blue eyes and leans down kissing her ever so softly, while grazing her scalp with his fingertips. She swoons underneath his touch. Ana grabs him by the hand leading him to the bed. She lies down under the blanket and waits for him to join her. Wren takes off his pants, dropping them where he stands then climbs into the bed next to her. She props herself up onto her elbows and turns to face him. She kisses him softly on the lips and smiles. She gently slides her hand down the side of his face looking deep into his eyes, as if to say thank you. Her hand travels down his neck and runs over the massive tattoo on his chest. It's an incredibly intricate piece of art that must have taken many sessions to do. It's a colossal image of an angry wolf wrestling with a serpent that wraps around the wolf's body. She traces the lines in the artwork and comes to a long piece of rough skin hidden in the design of the wolf.

She keeps coming back to that same spot until he stops her hand from running over it again.

"Please," he quietly pleads with her. She can hear the pain in his voice.

"I'm sorry," Ana apologizes, "Does it hurt?"

"Only the memories underneath it do," he confesses. Wren doesn't want to go into detail about the scar hidden in the ink but he knows it's going to bother her if he doesn't tell her something. He moves her hand from his chest to the bed so he can turn on his side and face her.

"It happened while I was working a little while ago. Not too long before I met you actually," he reveals. "It was bad. No one knew if I was gonna make it out of the hospital, and after everything that happened... this scar is the only thing that remains." He talks, touching the raised skin almost as if he's reliving the memory all over again. He closes his eyes turning away from her momentarily cringing at the thought of what he'd been through.

He sighs trying to get back into a better frame of mind and looks to her again, "Every time I looked in the mirror I would see it. Always thinking of the surgeries I had to have, how I almost lost my life, all of the therapy to get some form of normalcy back. I had it covered. The battle going on—" he rubs his hand over the entire piece, "it represents my constant fight to be the man I am now versus the man I was then. I don't mind you touching it, *me,* but I honestly can't take it when you move back and forth over it so much."

Ana listens intently as he opens up to her. She understands his pain of getting hurt on the job.

"I get it," she finally states remembering how badly she was recently hurt. And just like that the conversation about his scars, more emotional than physical, is over. Ana snuggles in close to him and he wraps his arms around her so they can fall asleep. In this moment she doesn't have a care in the world. She's not thinking about her sisters or her job. Right now, she doesn't even care if they find Nina Slade.

***

Nina and Sergio are banging on the door to Jeremy's apartment at eight in the morning. Nina turns to look at Sergio, who's irritation is growing since no one seems to be home. Nina picks up on this and assures him, "No worries... He's here. He just doesn't like to wake up this early."

"I'm not worried. Your life is on the line not mine," Sergio says to her just as Jeremy cracks the door enough for the solid steel chain to stop it from opening completely.

"Who the fuck are you? And whyyyyyy are you knocking on my door at this god forsaken hour?" Jeremy complains peeking through the space. Nina doesn't say anything; she just waits for Jeremy to recognize her. He squints and moves his neck from side to side. Then it hits him like a ton of bricks. He closes the door to remove the chain, then swings it open and throws his arms around his old roommate. "Get in here you crazy bitch! I missed you hun!"

Nina embraces her flamboyant friend while Sergio pushes past them right into the apartment. He draws his weapon, walking room to room, checking to see if anyone else is inside.

"Tell the Hulk over there…there's nobody else here but us. I sent my boy toy home hours ago. You know I don't sleep well with others," Jeremy stated to Nina with a laugh. She giggled a bit. She had been through so much lately she forgot how good it felt to be home. Sergio takes a seat on the couch and doesn't speak while Jeremy and Nina converse in the kitchen.

Jeremy looks at him, "Well aren't you the strong silent type!"

Nina responds to him, "Don't worry about him…he's just here to make sure I hold up my end of this deal."

"What deal?" Jeremy asks her.

"I made a deal with someone Jared owes money to in order not to be turned into a Russian sex slave, so we need to go to the bank like now. I gotta get back and I gotta find him. I need to bring him and the money to this guy or that's it."

"Well how do you plan on finding him, Ni- Eva?" Jeremy asks trying to keep himself from shattering Nina's alias.

"I left him a message to meet me at a spot when I get back next week. I hope he gets it."

"Oh he will honey no worries. So I see you put on some weight and changed your hair," he says sashaying around her flipping a few strands in the air. "Honey blonde looks good on you girl and so does all this thickness, I love it." He traces the curves of her silhouette with his hands.

"Thanks," Nina runs her fingers over her hair still a bit insecure about the new look. "I hope it's doing the job."

"Well I barely recognized you...so it's good for now."

"How much is left in the box?"

"Umm...I haven't dipped in there for a while. Something's been a bit off putting about the bank. But last time I checked it was over seventeen."

"Okay so let's go now, right when they open, so we can be in and out without too many people seeing us."

"Well how much are you taking out?"

"I need at least a hundred."

Jeremy gasps while dramatically clutching his chest, "Is that what saving your poon tang is worth these days? LORD... I need a vagina! But uhh…that amount of money being moved can't be done today. We have to go in and schedule an appointment to remove that much. They have to verify our IDs and all that shit."

"Damn it! I was hoping to get in and get out ASAP. The sooner I get back to Gabriel the sooner I can get back to living free."

"Is that what you call it? Living free?" Jeremy laughs at her attempt to glamorize living as a fugitive…*in Russia*! He shakes his head at his delusional friend and starts to move around the kitchen looking to make something to eat. "I'm starving. I can't believe you two assholes got me up and out of bed this early."

Sergio actually listens to that part and invites himself into the kitchen. He asks Jeremy if he would mind him whipping up something for everyone to eat. Jeremy doesn't object. About a half hour later, they are all eating a spectacular breakfast created by a bulky, gun toting Russian.

"Mmm. This is sooo good," Jeremy croons over his food. "You should cook professionally."

Sergio laughs, "I do. I'm the head chef at Tommy Jay's."

"Oh I definitely have to go back there now," Jeremy says kind of flirting with Sergio. However, the mention of the restaurant brings all kinds of memories back for Nina. She remembers sitting in the booth after Benjamin told her Mr. Aimsley was killed. She smiles to herself remembering the repetitive speech impediment he had that forced him to repeat the last word of his sentences twice.

"Something you want to share with us?" Sergio asks looking at Nina, who's smiling at her memories. Nina shakes her head no to Sergio's question and returns to eating her food. So much has happened and sometimes she misses Benjamin. She's almost sad that he got himself in the way. She wouldn't have had to kill him if he had just gone away after his car was vandalized. Even after David managed to put him in the hospital; he stuck around. No one's ever stood by her side the way Benjamin stood by for Blake. And after all she did for Xavier ... he left her for the goons. He didn't know what they would do to her, all he knew was that there was an opportunity for him to escape with his life and he took it with no regard to his so-called feelings for her. Nina continues on this train of thought; getting herself angrier and even more vengeful toward Xavier. She needs to get to the bank, so she can get back and deal with him.

The three finish up breakfast. Jeremy goes into his room to get dressed and ready to go to the bank. They decide to take Jeremy's car and never notice the car that begins to follow them. It always stays at least three cars behind and none of them recognize it on their way to the bank. Greg is driving too carefully, in Ana's opinion, while following Nina's old roommate, Jeremy.

"Seriously Greg?" she questions his driving ability, "Any slower and we'd be going backwards."

"Shut up! I just don't want them to see us."

"That's great but everyone sees us! It's like we're moving in slow motion. Let's go!"

"Chill out!"

"Just don't lose them! I wanna make sure we get some good shots of these two people with him. I'm sure one of them will lead us straight to Nina," Ana says finally getting excited about the assignment.

Her night with Wren was just the night of peace she needed to get her mind together. She's finally starting to become more at ease with the idea of letting her sister accept responsibility for her life and her actions. She hasn't told Anna Lee that yet, but she will sooner or later. Right now, she's focused on catching up to Jeremy and seeing who's in the car with him. They drive for a little while longer until they notice that Jeremy's already parked his car. He and the people with him are walking into a bank as Greg drives by.

"Shit Greg! I told you, you were driving too slow! Okay here's what we're gonna do. Let me out and I'm gonna walk up to the bank. You park across the street and when you see them coming out, give me a signal and get your camera ready. I'm gonna bump into them, making them stop long enough for you to snap their pictures. Don't waste the shots either; we're probably only going to get one chance at this."

Greg agrees to the plan. He sits across the street for about fifteen minutes and finally sees the big guy who was with Jeremy walking toward the door. He gets the camera ready and texts Ana, giving her the signal that they're coming. Ana walks fast pretending to be on her phone. She starts turning around in circles and looking up as if she's trying to locate an address on the buildings around her. She bumps right into Nina and Jeremy.

"Oh my goodness," Jeremy begins yelling, "Watch where you're going!"

"Oh I'm so sorry," Ana begins apologizing. She and Nina lock eyes, and for moment she gets flustered and taken aback by the subtle blonde's beauty.

"It's okay," Nina says to the Marshal, "May I say you have beautiful eyes?" Nina is also caught off guard by Ana's bright crimson curls, and stunning blue eyes.

"Thank you," Ana says with a smile. Ana thinks quick, trying to prolong this interaction so Greg can get their photos. "Hi my name is Ana. Do you know where Smith Street Boutique is?"

Nina smiles at her, "I'm Eva, and I believe it's about three blocks down and to the left." She points in the direction of which way Ana should walk. Ana thanks her and apologizes again for nearly knocking them down. She walks away in the direction Nina pointed her in and turns the corner to wait for Greg to drive around and pick her up. Greg finally comes around the corner, stopping the car for Ana to get in.

"Either you're a great actress, or the blonde made you blush," Greg says once she puts on her seatbelt.

"I have been classically trained, courtesy of the television for over thirty years," she says with sarcasm and a chuckle trying to hide the fact that she is smitten with Nina. "Did you get the pictures?"

"Yeah I got them. Here take a look." He hands her the camera for her to scroll through the photos he took. She stops at the picture he took of the beautiful blonde. She flips through the case file trying to compare the snapshot to the horrible image from Nina's identification badge from her job. The badge had some serious wear and tear on it after years of sliding in and out of electronic readers and Nina's pocket. Ana reads whatever notes are left on her from Nina's file at Brahman and Associates; but reads that Nina must have deleted her personnel file before she quit. Ana shakes her head at the flimsy research and goes back to the digital camera. She's stuck on her image unable to scroll past it. She wants to get to know this woman more. There's something about her.

"Well you were there for a bit longer than I anticipated. Did you get any vital intel?"

"Yeah the girl is Eva. I've never seen her before, but there's something about her I just can't put my finger on," Ana answers him.

Greg laughs, "Yeah it looked like there was something about her you'd like to put your finger on."

"Greg you're such a pervert!" she laughs playfully hitting him in the shoulder.

"I'm just saying there was a spark there. Anybody who saw the two of you together would say so," Greg observes. Ana shrugs her shoulders dismissing his thought, and he continues to drive back to the office.

***

"So what was that?" Jeremy asks Nina as he's driving back to his apartment.

"What was what?" she asks coyly.

"Even I saw that," Sergio says from the back seat.

"I have no idea what either of you are talking about," Nina laughs to herself.

"The red head... The clumsily bright red head...The girl with the curls!" Jeremy says getting excited.

"I don't know," Nina shies away from the questioning and turns her gaze toward the window.

"Uh, uh bitch, don't go mousy on me now! You and that red head sparked! Flames between you two, just as fiery as all that hair on her head! Can we go back and get her? Please Eva? You need some of her in you," he clears his throat with a chuckle, "I mean some of her in your life."

Sergio laughs quietly at him, and Nina continues to ignore Jeremy. She knew he was right though. There was something definitely up about that red head, Ana. *That's right, Ana is her name,* Nina thinks to herself. She had never considered being with a woman before, but something was drawing her to Ana. There is something magnetic between them, but she doesn't have the time to think about love right now. She needs to focus on getting this money back to Gabriel. She shivers at the thought of him stringing her up and skinning her like a side of venison.

They reach Jeremy's apartment. He parks his car and shuts it off looking at Nina and Sergio, "So what are you two going to do now? I have to go in to get ready for work."

"Why can't we stay here?" Nina asks seemingly offended. *I used to live here for goodness sake,* she thinks to herself.

"No offense to you handsome," he looks at Sergio through the rearview mirror, "but I just don't know you. And with whatever shit *she's* gotten herself into this time...I just don't need you bringing any extra *shit* into my space."

Sergio nods slightly shrugging his shoulders. He understands exactly what Jeremy means because he doesn't want Nina, and whatever *shit* she's into, coming home with him either.

Jeremy looks to Nina, "But you honey, can do whatever you like. Just let me know."

Jeremy doesn't really trust anybody except Nina. At least she's honest to him about the kind of person she is. She's a sociopath and as long as she's on his side, he doesn't care.

"Well, I can't leave the Hulk here," she tells Jeremy motioning her head in Sergio's direction.

"So I guess it's just you and me, stud muffin," she smiles devilishly at him and gets out of the car.

Sergio cringes at the sound of her calling him a pet name. He had wanted to avoid bringing Nina and her chaos into any of his personal space. It's bad enough she has already driven his car. Unfortunately, he has no other options. He follows her lead out of Jeremy's car and to his own, only parked a few spaces away.

Jeremy watches them drive off before going inside.

***

Sergio and Nina arrive at his house somewhere outside the city. He lives in a small ranch style house, but the land surrounding it is vast. You can see the top of a greenhouse behind his actual home. She is in amazement as she walks around his property. He was trying to get her to go directly inside, but her mind is wandering like a two-year-old in a toy store. She walks around back to get a closer look at the two-story structure that caught her attention as she walked onto the property. The greenhouse is massive. It's actually bigger than the house it's attached to.

"This is amazing! I've never seen anything like this," Nina gushes over the glass phenomenon.

"Thank you," Sergio says with a nod of his head, "I pride myself on what I take into my body, especially as a chef. I am very aware of what I need to sustain myself on this property...*alone.*" His emphasis on the word alone lets Nina know that she's intruding on a space that he doesn't like to share. She takes the hint; walking back around to the front of the house with him. They go inside, and he shows her to a guest room.

"I'm surprised you even have one of these. Just a moment ago it seemed like you prefer to be *alone*."

"I do, but with family and friends I prefer to sleep alone, so I had this added into the design when I built this place."

"You cook, you farm, you construct. You my friend are quite talented. Sounds like you stay pretty busy."

Sergio ignores her small talk. He just wants this time to pass so he can get back to his life. He walks over to a door and opens it showing her a lavish en suite. The bathroom has a glassed in shower, a huge claw-foot tub and marble countertops. The mirrors and vanity look vintage, but contrast well with the modern tile. His home looks like it was handpicked out of some country home and garden magazine. He leaves her inside the room. She doesn't hear him locking her inside of it though. She wouldn't care any way. She wants to get into that giant tub and soak her worries away.

She walks around the room peeking into closets and drawers to see if anyone left anything behind. But as she looks around she feels like she has been the only person to actually stay in the room. She shrugs her shoulders and falls back onto the big, comfy bed. Inhaling deeply, she can smell the fresh produce growing from his backyard. Nina is telling herself that she's going to get into that greenhouse at least once before she leaves. She begins to take her clothes off to get inside the tub.

She turns the bathwater on and waits while the water rises. She doesn't pour in any liquid to make bubbles, though. She hates bubble baths. Always has; and always will. Ever since she was a child she couldn't stand them, just like she can't stand Xavier. Thoughts of her lover plague her as the anger behind his cowardice grows each and every day. She stops the flow from the faucet and slides into the tub full of hot water. The steam coming off the water is beginning to turn her straight blonde hair into loose curly locks. Her tresses take her mind off Xavier and drift to images of Ana.

Those big blue eyes, and that bright red hair are permanently seared into her brain. She wonders if it's coincidence or fate that they bumped into each other at that moment. She sighs with a smile to herself.

Looking at the faucet, she sees the handheld body spray next to it. With ideas of how Ana must taste flooding her senses, she removes the handheld and holds it under the surface of the water to see if it works when she pushes the button for it to turn on. The spray causes multiple ripples and waves in the tub. She slides the body spray deep into the water until it's positioned directly in front of her pleasure. Nina spreads her legs open and slides down just a little to tilt her pelvis up into the flow of the body spray. She pushes the button. The first thrust of water against her clitoris is a bit rough so she maneuvers it until it's pushing the water against her anticipating womanhood. She pants as Ana's face flashes right before her eyes. She moans as she uses her fingers, spreading her lips to give the water a larger area of nerves to hit. It feels so good Nina feels like crying. She continues to move the sprayer up and down, increasing the intensity of her orgasm. Her pleasure pulsates with every wave of water and flash of Ana. She pants and cries out with her orgasm. "Ooh…," she breathes, "Ooooh…," she inhales, "Ooooh…," she pants, "Ooooh shit…," she inhales, "Ana…," she climaxes, "Ana."

Chapter 6

"Aaannaa," a tiny voice calls for her.

"Aaannaa," the tiny voice calls for her again. It is getting closer.

"AUNTIE ANABELLE!!" The tiny voice has found her in the kitchen talking to its mother.

"Yes my sweet Bella." Ana turns around to see why her darling niece has been calling for her.

"You said you would come play princess in the tower with me," the three-year old whines.

Anabelle looks at her sister, Anna Lee, who just shrugs her shoulders leaving her to make up an excuse as to why she hasn't come upstairs to play yet.

"Well my sweet Bella, I just came to talk to your mommy for a minute and then I have to go back to work. My partner will be here soon to get me. I just don't have time to play today sweetie," Ana tries to reason with the toddler.

"But-but-but when you called you said we can play when you come and I wanna I-I-I wanna play princess in the tower," she pouts to her aunt hoping to change Ana's mind about going to work.

Ana gets out of her seat and kneels down in front of her beautiful niece, strokes her hair and kisses her forehead. Her niece's big blue eyes were watering. It was like staring into a younger version of herself, even down to the curly red hair. "I'm so sorry Bella, I didn't know today was going to be the next time I was going to be here. But I promise you I'll come back this weekend and play with you all day."

Her face lights up, "Okay, see you this weekend Auntie Ana. And remember you can't break promises!" The toddler doesn't give her a chance to say anything else skipping out of the room.

"She's getting so big Lee," Ana returns to her seat to talk with her sister.

"I know time is flying. So what brings you here on a Friday morning? Oh my goodness you found Asia! Is she okay? Is she alright? Is she in the hospital?"

"Calm down Sissy. I found her, or she called for me rather. She was busted for possession and intent to distribute. I'm out of favors for her and the arresting officers aren't trying to give me any new ones."

Anna Lee wants to cry because she knows where this conversation is going and she knows there isn't anything that she can do about it. "Are you sure there isn't anything we can do? How about an attorney? Does she have a good lawyer?"

"Sissy you know damn well she can't afford a lawyer! She's getting a court-appointed defense attorney and that's it! We have to stop trying to save her, and let her save herself for a change. She needs to go to jail; hopefully she'll get sober."

"We can't just let her fend for herself! She's so easily manipulated, they'll railroad her! We need to get her a real lawyer! Soon Anabelle!"

Ana cringes as her sister calls her by her full name. She understands what Lee is saying, and actually agrees with her, but she has made herself okay with doing nothing for her sister. "I don't want to interfere anymore. The precinct handling it is already mad at me and she needs to learn her lesson. She can't always call me or depend on you to guilt me into helping her out every time she gets in over her head. This is her bed! She made it and now she has to lie in it!"

Anna Lee is quiet. She agrees with her sister but she doesn't want to let it go. She tries one last ditch effort to get her sister to help out, "Okay fine don't help! I'll just pull some money out of the bank and get her a lawyer myself."

Ana knows that the only money Lee has in the bank is the money she's putting away for Bella's future. She shakes her head but knows what she has to do, "No don't do that Sissy. I'll take care of it."

Anna Lee knows that was low to use her daughter's future to manipulate her sister, but Asia needs all the help she can get. And if Ana can't get her off, at least she'll have a better chance with a decent attorney at her side. Anna Lee is overjoyed that she is able to sway Ana to help out. She nearly jumps across the table to hug her oldest sister.

"Listen Sissy," Ana says unwrapping Anna Lee's arms from around her. "This is the last time. I'm going to put a call into a friend of mine to represent her. But this is it! And I'm telling Asia that too! The next time she gets into trouble she has to figure it out on her own. And I'm gonna make sure Jason knows that you're using Bella's future as a bargaining chip."

"Hey wait a fucking minute! There's no need for that! You know what we've been going through! This would make whatever pleasantries are left unbearable! Don't do that Anabelle!" Lee screams at her sister.

"Well then promise me the next time Asia gets into trouble you're going to let her fend for herself."

"Okay...fine. But you know the way Bella's account is set up we can't remove the money without an enormous penalty. I would never give her money to a junkie."

"Sissy, you're lucky I love you so much or I'd punch you right in the face!" Ana gets up from the table and brings the mug she was drinking coffee from over to the sink. She washes it out and places it on the dish rack to dry. She checks her phone to see Greg just messaged her to come outside. "Greg's here...I'll be back tomorrow to play with Bella, and you can go out with Jason or something."

"I don't think that'll happen, but okay Sissy," Anna Lee agrees reluctantly.

Ana leaves her sister's house and walks out to the car where Greg is waiting. She gets into the car so they can begin their day. She asks him about their tasks for the day to which he reveals that he wants to speak to Jeremy face to face. Ana doesn't think it's a great idea but Greg is under the impression that if he corners Jeremy, he'll get him to talk.

"But Greg that isn't standard operating procedure," Ana says worrying about his idea going wrong.

"This assignment isn't standard operating procedure, but here we are. Stop being such a pussy and let's do this! Let's get this over with. I wanna get onto another case already."

"Why the rush?"

"No rush; just want to get this done. Now we're gonna go to his job. I'll go inside to speak to him and you just stay in the car. I don't want him to get the idea that we're following him, it might spook Nina off."

"How do we even know Nina is still in contact with him?"

"We don't but that's what I'm going to find out. If he lies to me I'll be able to tell and if he's telling me the truth I'll be able to tell. Either way I'm gonna get something from him. Just stay in the car until I come out. We don't need him seeing you and getting suspicious."

Ana agrees, but can't figure out why Greg is in such a hurry to get through this case. She dismisses his attitude and sits quietly for the rest of the ride to Jeremy's job. Greg double parks across the street from the hair salon where Jeremy works. He walks inside the place which stinks of all kinds of chemicals.

The girl at the receptionist desk addresses him, "So what can we get for you today sir? Wash, trim, highlights?"

"Neither," Greg says flashing his badge. "What you can do is bring me Jeremy Eckles."

The receptionist takes one look at the badge and the blood leaves her face. She takes her pale cheeks into the back of the salon to fetch Jeremy. A few minutes later Jeremy emerges with an iced latté in one hand and his smock in the other. He shows Greg to the waiting area to have a seat on the sofa.

"So how can I help you today officer?" Jeremy asks while taking a sip from his coffee. Greg doesn't like him. Jeremy's demeanor; the inflections within his voice; his withdrawn body language… everything about him screams liar and snake.

Greg doesn't like him, "I'm looking for your roommate."

"Ugg! Not again! I went through all of this like a bazillion times already! I don't know where she is! I don't know where she went! And she didn't tell me where she was going!"

Greg looks at him, trying to read him and he seems to be telling the truth. He does try to shake him up though, "Well when you do see her, you'll be sure to let us know right? I mean you don't wanna be booked as an accessory after the fact or hit with interference with a federal investigation? Right?"

Jeremy's body shifted as if he was actually thinking about being locked up for helping Nina, but he keeps his cool. "I'll be sure to let you know as soon as I am in contact with her. Is there any other way I can help you do YOUR job?"

Greg is about to reply sarcastically when they hear a commotion going on outside of the salon. Apparently, a car nearly slammed into the car Ana is sitting in. She gets out of the car to move into the driver's seat, cursing out the driver and flashing her badge in the process. The other driver doesn't care about her badge, as he flips her off and speeds around the car. Ana isn't paying attention and unknowingly allows Jeremy to catch a glimpse of her moving around the car. Greg moves into Jeremy's line of sight distracting him from the mayhem going on outside.

"So you make sure you get in contact with me! Here's my card," Greg hands him a business card and leaves the salon.

Jeremy shakes his head at the Marshal and looks down at the card. He flicks it in the trash and goes back to work. He's anxious to see Nina later to tell her who's chasing after her now.

The day drags from that point for Jeremy. His last client finally leaves his chair. He cleans up and closes the shop down. Once he arrives home, Nina and Sergio are waiting for him in the hallway next to his apartment door. He rolls his eyes at Sergio, who's posted next to the door with his arms folded. Sergio does his typical sweep of the apartment.

Jeremy looks at him move room to room and finally speaks, "I still don't understand why you two just couldn't come in the morning to do this bank shit. It's not like I'm going anywhere."

"Well, the hulk over there doesn't like sharing! He couldn't stand the thought of someone else other than himself enjoying his house."

Sergio walks in at the end of her comment, "I like to enjoy the fruits of *my* labor. Besides whatever you're into, I don't want it coming to my house. So here is fine." Sergio takes a leather armchair from the living room and lodges it against the front door. He sits in it and closes his eyes while folding his arms across his chest. If Jeremy or Nina want to leave they have to go through him; literally. They shake their head at him and go into the kitchen.

Jeremy is nearly bursting at the seams waiting for Nina to ask him about his day. She keeps going on and on about Sergio's magnificent guest room and the enormous greenhouse in his backyard. He can't take it anymore, "Just shut up! Do you have any idea of who I saw and spoke to today?"

"No, why would I?" Nina asks.

"I spoke to a Greg McKinley today."

"Okay... Who the hell is that and why do I care that you spoke to him?"

"Well he's the U.S. Marshal that's been assigned to find you and bring you in," Jeremy brings his voice down to a murmur so Sergio can't hear their conversation.

"There are a few different agencies after me at this moment. You still haven't told me why I should care."

"Well you'll never guess who was riding shotgun with a badge of their own," he says with a smile wide enough to hide nothing.

Nina looks at him curiously, "Who?"

"Clumsy girl with all the curls."

"Ana?"

"Oh so you remember the red head's name? I thought you guys didn't have a spark?"

"We didn't! So what was she doing with the Greg guy?" she asks trying to distract Jeremy from his thoughts on her attraction to Ana.

"Greg is a Marshal, so I'm assuming that she is one too. She was in a car that almost got demolished outside the salon today. She got out to move it and that's when I saw those crimson curls. It was only a brief moment, but the dickhead cop got in my way before I could actually see her face."

"So you don't know that it was her?"

"You can hope and wish all you want honey, but those curls and that body are undeniable. It's too close that she bumps into us and then the next day I get a visit from the Marshal. I would bet he was in the car when she nearly knocked us down. We gotta hurry up and get you out of here!"

"Don't worry so much! We'll take care of the bank shit tomorrow morning and I'm on the flight back tomorrow night. Besides it's nice to know who's actively pursuing me. If I can get a little closer I may be able to *help* them with their investigation," Nina laughs.

"What the hell are you talking about? How do you plan on doing that?" Jeremy asks, confused.

"You don't worry about a thing. The less you know about what I got planned the less you can tell the Marshals when they come back to question you."

"How do you know they're coming back to talk to me?"

"Because you're the only true friend/associate that I had. They know we're in contact with each other, they just don't know that Eva is Nina. But they will soon enough. They'll know me in all my glory," Nina murmurs to herself. Jeremy snaps his fingers in her face to bring her out of the dark place she was going to. He thinks that there is something seriously wrong with Nina for wanting to get closer to the investigation and even play some kind of role, but he wasn't going to say anything else. He doesn't want to know anything else. The things that he knows she's capable of; already scare him. So whatever she has planned; he wants no part of it. They continue to talk into the night. The conversation is mostly about what Nina wants to do once the law stops chasing her. Somehow, Jeremy just doesn't believe that's going to happen but he goes along with the wishful thinking.

The following morning, the three of them go to the bank to withdraw the large sum of money Nina needs to bring back to Gabriel. Everything went as planned. There weren't any interruptions. There weren't any deviations from the plan. There weren't any meddlesome Federal Agents waiting to take Nina into custody. The extra weight she's put on along with the hair change has certainly bought her some time under the radar. She takes what she needs from the bank and leaves a significant amount in the safe deposit box. Nina walks out of the bank with a plan in mind. She's convinced that returning to the States just to see the investigation play out is exactly what she wants. But first things first, she needs to get back to Xavier.

Just like that she's back in the air, this time with Sergio on the flight with her. Back to Russia to settle a debt.

They land and walk outside of the small private airport. The weather is damp and cold just like the night they ran from Gabriel's goons. She's still in shock about how Xavier left her for them. Nina signals to the first driver sitting at the curb who pulls up in a black town car. Sergio is still quiet. He's been constantly looking over his shoulder as if they're being followed. Nina disregards his paranoid movements as they climb into their moderately luxurious transportation. She tells the driver to take them to a hotel not too far from where they are.

"Is there someone following us?" Nina asks him finally. The driver overhearing the question looks into the rearview mirror waiting for Sergio's response.

"No. Why do you ask?" Sergio answers her question with a question. The driver is pleased to hear that and shifts his focus back onto the road.

"You've been looking over your shoulder ever since you set foot off of the plane! You're starting to make me nervous!"

"I just don't like being here. Let's just get this over with so I can get back to my life."

"What happens when you're here that has you so paranoid?"

"That is none of your concern. Where are we going?"

"To pick up my bargaining chip," Nina answers him referring to

Xavier.

"Excuse me?"

"My husband, Jay...I need him and the money."

"How do you know he's going to be where we are going?"

"Because I told him to meet me there! He can't leave Russia without any money and he can't roam around owing Gabriel money either. He's waiting for me."

"How do you know he'll go with you to see Gabriel?"

"Well aren't you inquisitive all of the sudden?" Nina observes with a smirk. However, she knows his questioning is to divert all of the questions she has for him. This is the most conversation she's gotten from Sergio since he met her at the plane a few days ago. She shrugs her shoulders and continues to talk, "Jay is a greedy and needy asshole. He can't survive without me, so he will go where I tell him to, and he will do as I say."

Sergio looks at this woman next to him unsure of what she has planned. But one thing he is certain. He wants to get away from her as soon as possible. He's done his fair share of criminal activity, but he can feel the beast waiting to be released from underneath her façade. Something is definitely off-putting about her.

The towncar finally pulls up to a shabby hotel. There's a homeless man, hugging a bottle of vodka, using the building to hold him up. The homeless man reaches out his hand as Sergio walks by. At first Sergio is disgusted, but then takes a closer look at the man. His hands are nearly blue, cracked and scabbing all over. His coat is thin, and his boots are noticeably worn but seem to be the only piece of intact clothing he has on. Sergio takes off his gloves and his coat. He speaks to the man in their native tongue. He whispers some kind words to the drunk handing him the gloves and coat. Nina shakes her head and walks by them into the hotel. Sergio zips up the heavy Under Armor hoodie he had on underneath his coat and walks inside.

Sergio looks around the hotel lobby. It's dingy, rundown and in desperate need of a renovation. He doesn't want to touch anything and he doesn't want anything to touch him. He shakes off the creepy crawly feeling and begins to look around for Nina. She's nowhere to be seen.

He walks up to the front desk. The girl sitting there is barely coherent. He doesn't know what kind of drug she's on but knows she shouldn't take any more of it. He asks for Eva and the room she's in. The girl stares at him, blankly, as if she didn't understand what he was talking about. He asks again but this time describing what she looks like and the clothes she has on.

The girl refers to Nina as the American and holds out her hand.

Sergio looks down at her hand knowing that whatever he gives her will just end up being shot into one of her veins. But he needs to find her. He hands the girl about five U.S. dollars and she releases the information to him pointing him in the direction of the stairs with a room number.

Sergio takes the hike up five flights of stairs. He finally reaches the floor Nina is on and can feel something is wrong. He pulls out his Desert Eagle .44 caliber Magnum. Sergio walks quietly room to room, putting his ear to the door listening for Nina's voice with his finger on the trigger. He doesn't have to tip toe much longer as he nears the room at the end of the hall. He can hear Nina arguing with a man. Then he hears glass breaking and furniture being moved around the room. He reaches the door, which is wide open, just in time for a chair to smash and break against the wall outside the door. He takes a few quick breaths preparing himself to break up the battle going on inside the room.

Suddenly, the screaming stops and all Sergio can hear are repetitive grunts. He walks inside the room with his gun drawn; poised and ready to fire. He looks around at the chaos in the room. Money is all over the place. Then he sees that the briefcase it must have been in was sitting on the floor against the wall, snapped at the hinges. He sees the dent the briefcase made in the wall when Nina threw it at her target. He steps over the coffee table that now lies on its side. He walks around the corner from the living space into the bedroom. There's blood spray all over the walls. He continues to follow the sounds of the grunts.

As he gets closer to the sound, he hears mumbling in between the grunts. He follows the sounds along with the trail of blood toward the suite's bathroom.

He opens the door wide to see what's going on. He is expecting to see Nina hurt or getting hurt, but it's the complete opposite. Nina is covered in blood. Xavier is still on his feet, but barely. Nina is holding him up with one hand anchoring herself with one foot planted behind the other. She's looking down at her hand as it plunges the knife deep into his torso over and over again. Nina grunts every time the knife digs into Xavier's flesh. She curses at him every time she pulls it out. Blood spills out onto the floor every time she takes the knife out of his body. She is oblivious to Sergio's presence.

Sergio is horrified at the scene before him, but knows better than to show it. He's seen things like this before, but prefers his butchering to be done on livestock...not humans. He looks at her. She's getting tired. She can barely stand anymore. Xavier's eyes hold the cold look of death. Sergio tries to shake the look on his face from his memory like an etch-a-sketch. He holsters his gun, and walks closer to them.

"Eva," he calls lightly as not to startle her.

"I'm busy right now," she responds plunging the knife into his chest cavity with such force you can hear the sound of his breastbone cracking under the force.

"Eva I think he's dead now, you can stop," Sergio now pleads with her so they can get out of there.

"I know he is," she acknowledges with no emotion, "I felt his heart stop beating minutes ago. This, right now, is for my own pleasure."

Sergio looks at the disturbed woman, hoping to convince her to leave so they can go see his cousin. He tries again, but this time he moves behind her softly grabbing her by the wrist. "It's okay I'll take over."

"It's fine. I'm finished for now," Nina agrees to his gesture that's stopping her from using the knife anymore. The edges are jagged and even broken off in some areas. She lets Sergio hold up Xavier and take the knife from her hand.

"You need to clean up and we need to go," Sergio commands.

"I know but we need to bring him with us," Nina says motioning her head toward Xavier. She walks to the sink and turns the water on to begin rinsing the blood from underneath her fingernails.

"I can't carry a body out of here without someone seeing! We're just gonna have to tell Gabriel to come here or come back and get him later."

"Do you really believe *Gabriel* is going to come down here to this mess?"

"So what do you suggest?" Sergio asks, letting Xavier's body drop to the floor.

"Bring me a pillowcase and a trash bag," Nina orders. Sergio leaves the bathroom and returns shortly with the items she requested. "Now while I work on my situation in here, go out there and get the money together. Make sure it's all there too! Should be eighty grand in there."

Sergio doesn't argue with the blood-covered murderess. He goes out into the living room area and begins to pick up the scattered money. He looks all around the room, under the couches and under the flipped over table. He makes sure that every bill is accounted for because he wants this whole adventure to be done and over with. He just wants to get to Gabriel so he can get back home.

Chapter 7

Sergio isn't sure how much time has gone by since he finished counting the money and began straightening the room up. He just stares at the blood splatter on the wall. His compulsion for cleanliness is telling him to get some peroxide and bleach to clean it up, but considering the state of this hotel in general, it makes the compulsion pointless. He doesn't think any new guests would even notice the difference. He looks at the pattern reimagining that crazy bitch slicing the man she called her husband from ear to ear. Xavier's face of death flashes in his mind once again. He shakes the thought loose. He picks up the briefcase the money was in and examines it. He turns it a few times, upside down and then around to the back looking at the hinges to see if they're too mangled to be put back together. He looks up at the wall just above where the briefcase was lying, and runs his hands over the divot.

"Well, are you gonna put the money in the thing or just keep staring at the wall?" Nina asks from behind him, startling him out of his thoughts. He doesn't flinch.

He turns around to face her holding up the briefcase, "It's broken."

"So…fix…it," she replies walking by him smelling extremely clean for a murderer. He assumes she showered while he was getting the money together. She shakes her head and walks out of the room returning shortly with a roll of duct tape. She tosses it to him. He catches the roll and begins to put the rest of the money inside the case. He closes the briefcase, but the hinges won't let it close evenly. He wraps it several times in the duct tape. The thing looks so raggedy at this point that one would never know there was over fifty thousand dollars inside of it. Sergio finishes up and calls out to her asking if she is ready to go. Nina doesn't answer him but merely saunters out of the room with a pillowcase tossed over her shoulder. Sergio already knows what's inside of it. The thought makes him cringe.

They walk out of the hotel room, down the stairs and out of a back door. They should have some time before anyone notices the mess Nina left in the bathroom. Stepping out into the cold air instantly reminds Sergio he gave his coat to that homeless man out front. Nina shakes her head, "You're way too nice! Quiet, but nice. I would have never gave that man anything."

"Well there lies the difference between you and I then," he remarks knowing there is a shitload more that separates the two of them. They hustle down the street to hail a taxi. One comes along rather quickly to Sergio's delight. He tells the driver to take them to Gabriel's Garden. Nina rolls her eyes at the mention of their destination. It doesn't take long for them to arrive and they are greeted immediately.

Sevastian is the one to show them into an office-type room. This room is completely different from the one Nina was initially held in when she was brought here. This room is warm, with sixteen feet high ceilings and marvelous wood carved moulding tracing the creases where all of the corners meet. Three of the walls are lined with shelves that must house over a thousand books in several languages. There is a desk, near the back wall which contains no shelving, just three massive floor-to-ceiling windows. The desk is solid, a beautiful dark cherry, and it sits in front of the center window. The curtains behind it are drawn but don't meet in the middle, allowing a meager glimpse of the city skyline to enter the room. There are two chairs, upholstered in a soft midnight blue fabric, in front of the desk. That's where Sevastian tells them to wait. Sergio takes a seat but Nina is so overwhelmed by the magnitude of wealth in the room, she can't sit down.

She places her pillowcase by her chair on the floor and tells Sergio to put the briefcase on the desk. He does as she asks, while she walks around running her fingertips over the spines of every book she can touch. Gabriel doesn't stop her when he walks in but instead goes straight to Sergio to greet him. Sergio rises out of his chair. They grab each other by the forearm and move in close for a brotherly embrace. Gabriel smiles but Sergio is unable to.

"Is something the matter cousin?" Gabriel asks him. His deep voice travels through the room, striking Nina right inside her eardrum making her aware of his presence. She stops molesting his books and makes her way back to the seat Sevastian showed her to. Sergio looks his cousin in the eye, "All will be well as soon as this task is complete." Gabriel nods his head, understanding how hard Sergio has been trying to stay out of trouble.

"Would you like a drink Sergio?" Gabriel asks moving toward his liquor cabinet that is built into the book shelving.

Sergio declines and returns to his seat.

"How about you, my Daphne?"

Nina agrees and takes the glass of liquor from Gabriel's hand. She looks at him differently from the first time she met the gangster. She knows the beast of his true nature but has discovered her own; yet again. She respects him, but still fears him. She won't be able to let that fear go until she knows her debt is paid. She drinks the glass of vodka in one swallow. She waits for Gabriel to sit down behind the desk and moves the pillowcase from the side of her chair to in front of her feet.

Gabriel finally sits down looking at the rickety briefcase placed on his desk with a raised eyebrow. He turns it around without lifting it off the desk. Nina looks at him apologetically for its appearance. Gabriel makes a slight hand gesture acknowledging her silent apology. He calls for Sevastian. He tells Sergio to go with Sevastian to take the briefcase to a place he calls "The Vault." Sergio doesn't argue, he just gets up and does as he is told. He leans over the desk and whispers something to Gabriel.

Gabriel's response, "That's very good to know," he strokes his beard. "We'll be in touch cousin, just keep an eye on it for me until I get there."

Nina is quizzical about what Sergio told him but dares not question either of them. She watches as Sergio straightens his hoodie and walks away with Sevastian. Once the two men leave the room, Nina is alone with Gabriel once again.

"You didn't count it," Nina speaks up a bit disappointed.

"There is no need to count it. You would not dare short me. No one ever has and those who have tried, weren't alive long enough to speak of it. So I know you brought me the money, but isn't there someone missing from this equation? Where is he?"

"He is here," Nina says nonchalantly. She reaches for the pillowcase at her feet, grabs it and stands up placing it on his desk. The pillowcase covers a black trash bag. She moves the pillowcase down to the base of the bag. Nina whips out her knife, the same one that killed Xavier, and moves it across the top of the bag under the knot. Gabriel stares into the cold dead eyes of Xavier's face. He has no expression looking at the head of this man who annoyed him so much. Nina, however, is smiling ear to ear, eager to tell Gabriel of her conquest.

"Please sit," Gabriel tells her. She sits back down pouting like a toddler, visibly upset that Gabriel hasn't acknowledged her achievement. He summons one of his girls to come in and remove the head from his desk. He tells her to add it to his collection. Nina imagines what that room must look like with a maniacal grin creeping across her face. He stares at Nina sitting in front of him. Her grin disappears as she refuses to look him in the eye. He gets up to move around the desk, positioning himself right in front of her.

"My beautiful Daphne...so delicate, so deadly. Please tell me your name," he requests in a softer tone than she is used to.

"You know my name. It's Eva, Eva Sloane," she answers sarcastically at first but mellows her tone remembering who she is speaking to. He nods his head in agreement with her speech adjustment.

"We both know that is a lie. I am in the business of knowing when people lie to me," he says while stroking his beard, "So I will only ask you this one more time...what is your name?"

She closes her eyes, "It's Nina."

"You are something remarkable, Nina. I knew you were going to kill your lover, but I didn't know it would be with such ferocity. You surprised me and that never happens."

She blushes slightly at the accolades she's finally receiving. Nina finally looks up into Gabriel's eyes. There's a glimmer in his eye that she has never seen. Suddenly, the fear that used to bear down over her has turned into an unbridled attraction. The scar traveling down the left side of his face does nothing but make him even more attractive to her. Her heart starts racing.

He breaks into her thoughts, "Stand up Nina."

She does as she's told. Even with her standing, he still towers over her.

"Let me see you," he commands. He makes a gesture with his hand which signals her to undress.

She does as she's told.

"Very very nice," he says eyeing her in her bra and panties. "I am almost sad that you could not be one of my flowers," he reveals, still leaning against the desk.

Gabriel's Garden is full of broken women, who will not use their voices to resist his command. He breaks them down individually, first mentally, and then physically. He subjects them to the calm fear he embodies, and once it is instilled within their bones, he samples them all finding their best and worst assets. He itemizes the qualities that will intrigue his special clients. His business sense is expansive, and seemingly wasted in the life of crime he chose for himself. He looks at Nina wanting to find her qualities. He knows he can break her but it would take much longer than the others and he would lose many men and clients in the process. He decides that a mere sample should be enough to satiate the loss of what could have been his best flower in the garden. He looks at her, "Come here."

She does as she's told.

"Open your mouth," he tells her.

She does as she's told. He palms the back of her head, running his fingers through her short hair, and yanks her head back. She grunts quietly. His slender build disguises his true strength well. She can feel the brute force hiding behind his slim figure.

"Don't you make a fucking sound!"

She does as she's told. In a matter of seconds, Gabriel has his tongue in her mouth swirling around hers; tasting the vodka they had both drank. Nina is so deep into the kiss she forgets what kind of man Gabriel is. She moves her hands up from her side to hold his arms. The moment she does that he breaks their lip lock. His hand is still entangled in her hair as he moves his free arm across her body, gets up from the desk, spinning her around, so now he is directly behind her with her arm pinned to her back. It all happens in one swift motion. She grimaces in the pain, but is still turned on.

"You move when I tell you to move," he speaks in her ear. His voice is deeply masculine and she can feel his breath and his beard on her skin. She nearly melts at its sound. He still has her pinned, bent over the desk, and his voice snarls when he says, "And don't fucking touch me." He jerks her forward just a bit forcing her to hit her hip bone on the edge of the desk and her shoulder to twist in pain.

He finally releases the grip on her arm and hair. Gabriel allows her to turn around to face him again. Her eyes are watery but she refuses to let a tear drop. She clenches her teeth, staring him in the eyes to let him know that he just hurt her. But Gabriel doesn't care. This moment isn't about passion, it isn't about love, and it isn't about trying to build a new relationship. This moment for him is about touching the deepest part of this woman. A woman so like himself. This woman is just as ruthless as he is and he wants to feel the very depth of her tormented soul.

He places her hands, which are folded in front of her, by her sides on the edge of the desk. He uses one foot to nudge her feet wide apart. He wraps his hand around her throat tightly to hold her in place while he rips her panties off. Her skin shows bright red streaks from where the fabric was torn away. Nina is so entranced by his charisma, his dominance; she doesn't see or hear him unsheathe his manhood. She doesn't look at it; her eyes never leave his.

"Open your mouth," he commands her.

She does as she's told.

Gabriel places two of his fingers on her tongue. Nina sucks them gently. He removes his fingers from her mouth and uses them to graze the flesh between her legs. He runs them from the back of her pleasure to the top and around her clit. Then he slips them inside of her. Her walls tighten around his fingers, which intrigues him, it excites him; his manhood is pulsating with anticipation. He strokes himself while stroking her. He takes his fingers out of her and sticks them back into her mouth. She licks her own juices off his skin. The very act of her enjoying this moment makes him more curious about the kind of being that she is.

His sense of urgency to be inside of her grows. His pulse quickens as she continues to suck his fingers sensually. She eyes him seductively. *Enough with her teasing*! With one hand grasping her waist, he snatches his fingers from her mouth. He wraps them around her throat. He squeezes tightly and angles her back to hold her in place. He plunges himself deep inside of her. The first thrust is so powerful it forces her back and up onto the desk. He strokes her forcefully, mercilessly. The only sounds are the barely audible grunts he utters with each push. He pumps a few more times. Nina struggles to breathe as Gabriel fucks the life from her. Every stroke he squeezes tighter. Every breath is harder to take. Her lungs cry for air with each and every thrust.

Nina begins fading out of consciousness when she feels wetness underneath her cheek. She glimpses down at the desk to see that some of the blood, from the trash bag Xavier's head was in, had spilled onto the desk. She was sitting in it. It was smearing with every stroke. It revives her. It invigorates her! It steals her attention! Her eyes darken with lust.

Gabriel is distracted as Nina is no longer in the moment with him. He looks down to see what she's looking at. He sees the blood. It excites him too, making him loosen his grip around her throat. He fucks her faster, harder. Nina looks at it smearing all over the desk, smearing onto her thigh, and grows excited with every thrust. She slides her hand in it and then reaches up touching Gabriel. She rubs the blood on his neck right under his chin. He releases her throat, grabs her hand and slams it back down into the blood. He's infuriated that she has disobeyed him! His other hand moves up to the back of her neck while the hand that splattered in the blood comes up quickly and across her jaw. The slap stings as Xavier's blood drips down Nina's face. Not once did Gabriel stop fucking her.

He pumps a few more times, getting more and more forceful with every movement. Nina tries to brace herself moving her hand back out of the blood inadvertently placing it on the knife. The same knife she killed Xavier with… the same knife she used to cut the bag open revealing his severed head. Her heart starts racing as her fingers grip the handle. Gabriel is just about to climax when he takes his eyes off of her, looks up at the ceiling, and suddenly feels the jagged edge of the blade in his side. The knife ripping into his torso brings her to climax. He pulls out of her immediately falling back onto the velvet covered chair as her juices drip down his shaft.

Nina is wide eyed looking at Gabriel bleeding onto the chair but he's still hard. She moves off the desk and falls to her knees. She takes all of his manhood into her mouth and sucks him vigorously. The pain, the adrenaline, the orgasm; they're all hitting his senses at once. His nerves are going crazy and he doesn't know what to do. The feeling is unbearable…she orgasms again. He feels like he's about to explode. And then… he does. He releases his fluid into her mouth while pulling the knife from his side and stabbing it into the arm of the chair. The release is soothing.

Gabriel is panting, "Get dressed." He unbuttons his shirt to look at the injury.

Nina does as she's told. She isn't sure what Gabriel feels toward her at this moment. "I apologize," she begins, "I got so caught up in the moment…I didn't mean to hurt you."

"Do not lie to me Nina," he reminds her, still out of breath. He tells her to go in his desk drawer and get the black bag that lies in it. She gets the bag and opens it for him as he is still gripping the site of his wound. He rummages through the bag. He pulls out two small, glass containers and a syringe. He injects the liquids from both vials directly into the gash. He growls in pain as he stuffs gauze, that he douses with some kind of disinfectant, into the open flesh. He patches the area and then seals it with a large bandage and medical tape. All Nina can do is stand back and watch as he repairs himself.

"You're like a robot," she says. She meant to say it in her head, but it came out unexpectedly.

He snickers and then cringes in pain, "I just know how to deal with battle blows. My beautiful Daphne, you are exactly who and what I thought you are. Deadly…but luckily for me; I am not easily killed. As you can see." He traces his finger over the large scar on his face. She can only imagine what must have happened to the person who did that to him. His hand then rests under his chin. He starts stroking his beard. He feels the blood drying, and getting sticky on his neck.

"I told you not to move…I told you not to touch me."

"No one told you to fuck me! On a desk covered in blood no less!"

He stands out of the chair and slaps her again, a quick lash across her face that still has traces of blood from the first time he struck her.

Nina's face is hot. It sears with pain as she feels the welts developing. She knew better than to speak to him in that tone. She had gotten too comfortable and for some inexplicable reason felt they were equal. They both look at the mess they made. He calls in Lana to clean it up. Nina just stands there and watches silently, knowing not to speak of anything while she is in there. The old woman finishes up rather quickly, as if she's used to cleaning up blood.

"You will mind your tone when speaking to me. This will be your last warning," he backs away from her as if nothing is wrong putting his shirt back on. She looks at him as if he has three heads.

That was a warning? she thinks to herself still touching her cheek. She becomes fearful of what he would do to her had she angered him completely.

He responds to her facial expression, "I am built strong. I like you. I respect you. Even though I do not tolerate the way your lips speak so loosely to me; it takes some serious gall to stab someone. To get up close and personal. To feel the flesh split as the blade slides through. Anyone can shoot from far away. But to take a life with your own hands. To feel it slip away from your target. To see that last breath be taken. You and I are one in the same.

Your debt to me is paid. Go and meet Sergio at the airport. You will not come back to Moscow… ever! This incident," he motions toward the area where she stabbed him, "does not go unnoticed. It goes on the books and if I see you in my presence again…I will kill you where you stand."

"I—," Nina begins to talk.

He holds up a finger to hush her. "Do not speak. Just go before I change my mind."

Nina doesn't utter another word. She grabs her jacket and the rest of her belongings running out of the room. She fought with the devil and won. *This place will be behind me very soon,* she thinks as she walks out into the street looking for a taxi. She disposed of Xavier. She did battle with a beast, but got fucked by a thug. She managed to get banned from a country but escape with her life. She makes it to the small airport where Sergio is already on board. She sits down in a seat across the aisle from him. He looks at her and shakes his head.

"What?" she asks cocking her head to the side.

"Nothing. It is none of my concern."

"Seriously, speak your mind," she pushes.

"I don't know who you really are Eva, or what you did. But you managed to owe Gabriel money, use his private plane twice and leave his presence unscathed. You have to be some type of crazy. Those are the only kind of people, outside of his family, that he respects. Those are the only kind of people he allows to live."

"Well not completely unscathed," she turns for him to see the welts of Gabriel's fingers across her face, "But what difference does it make to you what kind of crazy I am?" she asks him as they take off into the air and back to the States.

"It doesn't. I just don't want it infiltrating my life. I love my cousin, but he is the craziest and the scariest son of a bitch I have ever known. For you to be okay with him and not be related to us means that you're not too far off kilter from him. Somehow I feel that whatever shit you're wrapped up in, dealing with my cousin is the tip of the fucking iceberg. When we get back to the States my dealings with you are done."

"No problem, Sergio. Your dealings with me are done," Nina agrees. She turns over to look out the window. He turns over and falls asleep for the first time in days. He knows that should she do something to him, Gabriel would take his time taking her life, so he feels comfortable closing his eyes around the murderous beauty. Nina falls asleep not too long after he does. The flight goes smooth and so does the landing. Luckily for them, the plane lands at a tiny airstrip just outside of the city. Nina has Jeremy meet her there. He walks up to greet them as they get off the plane. Sergio ignores him and walks away from them hoping that it's the last time he has to see either one of them.

Jeremy turns his face up at Sergio's rudeness, "What the fuck is his problem?"

"He doesn't want to deal with my crazy," Nina answers.

"Say what? Come again?"

"The Hulk over there thinks I'm crazy and doesn't want any of it leaking into his life."

"Oh well that's okay, we don't want to leak into his life anyway," Jeremy says sarcastically.

"You're absolutely right, I want to leak into the red head's life," Nina smiles mischievously.

"You're still on clumsy girl with the curls...who's really a Marshal looking for your ass?"

"I gotta make sure they tell my story right. I gotta have some kind of influence on this investigation. As soon as I get them off my trail, I'll disappear...and for good this time. I'll go somewhere warm and tropical. No more winter nights, no more frozen walks in the snow, no more run-ins with gangsters and cowards. Just white beaches and fruity drinks."

"Oh can I come with, or wait? Is Xavier coming too? He's such a buzz kill," Jeremy whines.

"No worries, Xavier won't be killing anyone's buzz anymore. He got caught up in Moscow and won't be leaving any time soon."

"Is that right? So what about the thug trying to sell your poon tang?"

"He's done with me as well. Our business is done, and I will not be a flower in Gabriel's Garden!"

"Okay well let's get the fuck out of here then."

"Yes...let's."

Jeremy and Nina get into his car to go back to his house. Flashes of her killing Xavier and stabbing Gabriel bring up memories of her shooting Benjamin in the head. She misses him again. She thinks about that long day they worked side by side in the archive warehouse. She remembers him coming to her rescue on a drunken night. She remembers the sincerity of his voice when he told her he would always come to her aid. She misses him again. She wishes he hadn't got in the way. Shaking those thoughts loose from her head; she tries to refocus on her next task.

She needs to find a way to get to Ana. She wants to get close to her, she wants Ana to fall in love with her. She wants that wet dream she masturbated to in Sergio's huge bath tub to turn into reality. She realizes that Ana doesn't know who she is right now or they would have swooped in at the airport to take her into custody. Hell, they would have taken her at the bank. Nina feels like there's still a small window for her to have a little bit of fun before she goes out with a bang. But first she has to find her way in.

How is she going to work her way into Ana's close circle? Who can she use to infiltrate her most intimate spaces? The questions circle her mind as they drive back to Jeremy's house. Traffic is light but not too light for either of them to notice the car following them home from the landing strip.

Greg has been tailing Jeremy ever since he left the salon that day. Ana isn't with him, so he won't interact. He's maintaining a safe enough distance but he wants to get a better look at the honey blonde bombshell. He knows that there is more to her than just a friend visiting from out of town. He just doesn't know it yet. He wants to get closer to her, but knows he needs Ana as his way in. He just wants to know who is the mysterious girl who has taken Nina's place as Jeremy's new "BFF"?

Who is she?

"Who is she?" Greg asks... talking to no one, "Who the fuck is she?"

Chapter 8

"WHO THE FUCK IS SHE?!"

"Anna… Please…calm down baby. It's not what you think it is."

Jason's tone with his wife, Anna Lee, is calm which does nothing but anger her more.

"DON'T TELL ME TO CALM DOWN! WHO THE FUCK IS THAT WOMAN LEAVING MESSAGES ON THE ANSWER MACHINE LIKE IT'S OKAY?! WHO. THE.FUCK.IS.SHE?"

"Babe, I promise you that it's no one important. There isn't anything going on. I'm not having an affair or anything like that," Jason tries to reason with Lee; but it doesn't seem to be working.

Wren is dropping Ana off at her sister's house as the argument gets heated. All Ana can hear as she walks up the path to the front door is her sister yelling at someone and then something being thrown and shattering. She draws her weapon and approaches the door, which is partially opened. She steps into the hallway that leads to an opening into the living room and further down are the stairs leading to the second floor. Ana steps into the doorway of the living room. Jason and Anna Lee stop talking and look at Ana like she has seven heads. Ana quickly holsters her weapon.

"What the hell is going on in here? I can hear you all the way out on the street!" Ana shouts at them angrily.

"Never mind what's going on in here! What the hell is wrong with you coming in our house with your weapon out? Bella is here Sissy!!" Anna Lee yells to her sister.

"Well the way you two were going at it I didn't think she was. Where is she?"

"She's upstairs Anabelle," Jason tells her with a breath of exhaustion.

Ana doesn't stay downstairs to listen to their argument, but instead decides to go up to Bella's room and check on her niece. She opens the door to the pink paradise. Her sweet niece is sitting on a velvety pink ottoman, with headphones on that are almost bigger than her little head. Ana chuckles to herself as she walks up to her little princess. Bella is singing along to her favorite Disney movie, Frozen. She is so into the movie she doesn't hear her aunt walk into the room. Ana removes the headphones from Bella's tiny ears.

"Hey! I was listening to that," Bella whines turning around to see who interrupted her movie. She is overjoyed to see her aunt standing there. "Auntie Ana! Auntie Ana! You came back to play with me!"

"I sure did kiddo, but I see we're watching a movie."

"Yeah," Bella's face gets a little sad, "Momma and Daddy are talking too loud again. Can you watch it with me? I just want to watch it one more time. Pretty please???"

"Absolutely Bella, but let's not use the headphones. Let's turn the TV all the way up, and let's *sing* all the songs," Ana partially sings to her niece, scooping her up off the ottoman and twirling her around in the air. The little girl laughs and screams with every spin. Bella has a very special place in Ana's heart since she doesn't have any children of her own. She hates how her sister gets so wrapped up in her husband that she forgets about her daughter being there listening to every slanderous and hurtful word.

The two of them run, play and sing for hours until little Bella passes out.

Ana tip toes out of her room and back downstairs where her sister and her husband are finally speaking with their inside voices.

"Do I even wanna know what it was about this time?" Ana says walking into the living room.

Jason starts, "I was just trying to help and the whole thing got blown way out of proportion as it always does!"

"Way out of proportion?!" Anna Lee interrupts her husband. "Wait Sissy just listen," Lee gets up and presses play on the answer machine.

"Hey Jay, I got what you need baby. Lost your cell call me back," a sultry voice plays off the tape. Ana listens to the message and can understand why her sister would get upset but not why that message brought on World War Three. She shoots Jason a look for him to explain the message.

He responds to Ana's glare, "I'm gonna tell you just like I told Lee, it just sounds bad. But I'm not gonna defend myself to the both of you every time Lee has a fucking conniption! Lee...you are my wife! And I wouldn't do anything to betray our bond! The woman on the machine is someone who is trying to help me help you guys."

"Huh?" They both look at him confused.

Jason sighs and begins to explain, "When Asia got locked up, you were so devastated and then you telling me how Belle is out of favors; I felt like I had to do something. I know I'm just a paralegal but I asked a few people around the DA's office about the case and I was given the name of a young woman who might have some information that could help Asia. That was her calling me back. She said she lost my cell so that's probably why she called the house. We can call her back right now so you can see for yourself."

Ana and her sister exchange glances questioning whether or not they should take him up on his offer. "Dial the number," Lee demands.

"And put it on speaker," Ana chimes in.

The phone rings a few times until the same sultry voice answers, "Hello?"

"Hey Kaley, it's Jason, I got your message."

"Oh hey baby, listen the girl you were asking about. She did have the brick in her hand but she went in the back room with Junk. When the cops raided the place; the brick wasn't in the room because I had it and was already choppin it up. But I can't be talkin about this right now. I got a deal goin myself and can't fuck it up."

"Okay but if you tell the DA about Asia, will that hurt your deal?"

"I don't know cuz the dude she went in the room with was an undercover but he sure wasn't actin like it."

"How do you know he was a cop?"

"Because I'm his C.I. and I'm the one who got him set up with Danny's crazy ass. But they need her to get to Danny. I'm pretty sure somebody'll cut her a deal."

"Okay thanks Kaley, I owe you."

"No problem. How about you tell your wife to make me some more of that lasagna you gave me that day? I didn't mean to eat it all, but it was really good." There's a brief pause and they hear her talking to someone in the background, "It's okay baby, I'm getting off the phone in a minute. I'll take care of it." She returns her attention back to the conversation with Jason, "Yeah so some of that lasagna would be great. The food in this home sucks."

"Okay Kaley, I'll definitely do that for you. I'll talk to you soon."

"Okay Jay, later baby."

He hangs up the phone and looks at the two sisters just sitting there.

"I'm so sorry baby, I just heard the voice and I thought the worst. I'm so sorry," Lee begins spewing apologies to her husband. She gets up from the seat next to her sister and goes over to her husband falling to his feet, and hugging him around his knees.

"Don't apologize for how you feel. Ever! The only person you need to apologize to is our daughter. She was here to hear all of that and she shouldn't have had to. Next time you have an issue with me, you wait until you can have a calm conversation."

All Ana can do is nod her head in agreement with her brother-in-law.

"And Ana," Jason turns his attention to her, "Please stop snooping on me for her. You never find anything, and you never will because I have not and WILL NOT cheat on my wife. I have a bit more respect for our union than she does."

Lee gets up, feeling the sting of that last remark. Her husband was right about that. If she can't trust him then she can't respect their marriage.

She sits down next to him, and looks at Ana. "I'm gonna tell the both of you something that has been eating me up inside. I know...Jason. I know about the affair you had two years ago. I never said anything but because I never resolved it with you I haven't been able to trust you which is why I get so crazy at the littlest things."

Ana looks over to Jason waiting for him to deny it, but he doesn't. He sits quiet for a moment before asking her how she found out. Lee tells them that it was right after Bella was born, and she could tell that

Jason's heart and mind weren't at home. It was something that she could feel.

Those feelings were validated one day when someone slid an envelope under the door. There was a letter and a few pictures of Jason and the other woman. It wasn't anything scandalous but you could see the chemistry between them in the pictures. The letter went on to explain how long their relationship was going on for, which had only been a few weeks, but the other woman thought it was serious because it wasn't just sex for them. They had a bond and spent most of their time just talking. The letter said that the affair was over, but the woman's conscience was eating her up so badly that she had to let her know about her husband just in case he decided to move on to another mistress. The letter told Anna Lee to leave her husband, but Anna was paranoid thinking that's what the woman wanted... to leave her husband so she can have him. She didn't know what to do, so that's when she started calling Ana to play private investigator for her. Although it wasn't too private if Jason was aware of her following him around. The letter, and pictures of them out for dinner weren't enough evidence for Lee, she wanted the dirty details. She wanted pictures of them intimately. Yet, every time she had a hunch or Jason came home with signs that he had been up to no good, there was never any evidence left behind.

Jason's hands are folded, resting on the bridge of his nose, with his elbows pressing into his knees. All he can do is look down at the floor and shake his head in shame. He thought he had covered his tracks from that affair so well; he never anticipated Claire ratting him out. He explains to them that the time was rough, between things he had going on at work and the new baby at home, he wasn't sure of what he wanted to do.

Then one day out of nowhere, his beautiful wife and daughter came to visit him for lunch at the office. Everyone oo'ed and aahh'ed at his little princess and his beautiful wife. His wife who had brought him lasagna. He suddenly appreciated just how lucky he was to have them as a family, and broke it off that day. He never led the girl to believe that he was ever going to leave his family, but he was sure that the thought crossed her mind, especially as she wrote the letter to Anna Lee. He thought he was being so careful because he never wanted Lee to find out or get hurt. He thought they could just rebuild what they had. He never knew that the letter was the reason behind Lee's crazy antics.

"You two deserve each other," Ana states after listening to the both of them, "I've never known two people who've loved each other more than the two of you. You guys have been together what? Eleven years now, married for four, dating since middle school. If you two don't want to be together then don't be together! You keeping secrets from each other has done nothing but make all of our lives crazy!

"Sissy I love you, but like I said before, if I didn't love you so much I'd punch you in the face. You got me out here looking crazy investigating my brother-in- law for shit that happened two years ago that you couldn't let go of. And you! You son of a bitch! You got my sissy going crazy out here because you couldn't handle life! I get it! But shit happens! You don't just step out of something so sacred and so special because you're confused! You're supposed to go to her, and Sissy you need to be open for him *to* come to you!

I'm done with this. My PI days are over, and from now on I just wanna be Auntie Anabelle."

Ana gets up from the couch feeling emotionally drained when her phone starts going off. "Okay guys that's work, I gotta go. Can't be playing Dr. Phil in here all day. Are you guys going to be okay?"

Anna Lee gets up from the couch and hugs her sister tightly. Ana can feel the relief in her hug that they're going to be okay. She says goodbye to Jason and leaves the house.

Once, she's outside she calls Greg to come pick her up at her sister's house. He lets her know that the honey blonde, who they saw that day with Jeremy, is back, but not the big guy. They still haven't been able to identify the blonde yet. They can only assume that she is the Eva Sloane person he has been communicating with. And Eva Sloane is as clean as a whistle. Ana could care less about that or anything else right now, much less work. She just wants to go unwind and have a drink. Greg gets to Ana in about a half hour. They go to their regular after work spot and start drinking and talking.

Greg got so caught up in getting to Ana that he completely dismisses the fact he was tailing Jeremy. So when he pulls off to go to her, Jeremy notices him and begins to follow him. Jeremy follows Greg all the way to Anna Lee's house, making sure he isn't as obvious as Marshal McKinley. He watches as clumsy girl with the curls gets into the car that had been following him around these last few days. When they leave, he waits a minute or two and then leaves his space making sure to keep them in his sights. He follows them to the pub. He calls Nina and tells her to get down to that bar as soon as possible.

Greg watches Ana drink beer after beer until her vision is blurred and her judgment's impaired. Greg never gets as drunk as she does. He often has half of a beer and then three bottles of water to piss it all out. He looks at his inebriated partner and asks her if she wants him to call Wren for her. She tells him to do that so he can go home to his wife; she doesn't want his wife to be mad at her for keeping him out. Greg texts Wren, from Ana's phone, to tell him where they're at so he can come pick her up. Wren texts back a few minutes later to say he's on his way. Greg takes that as his cue to leave. He tells Ana to make sure she texts him when Wren gets there. She tells him okay and Greg leaves to go home.

The next person to talk to Ana, however, is a short honey blonde, with a slightly thick body. Ana looks at Nina with a smile as she approaches her at the table.

"Hey I know you," Ana says to her before she can even sit down.

"And I know you too, clumsy girl with all of those crimson red curls," Nina says to her twirling one of her fingers in a loose curl hanging by Ana's face.

"I'm Ana."

"I remember," Nina says with a seductive smile, "I'm Eva."

"I remember," Ana replies obviously drunk. "So what are you doing in here? Are you following me?"

"I should be asking you that."

They both laugh.

"No, seriously…what are you doing here?" Ana asks her again, this time touching the top of Nina's hand softly. The motion itself is brief, but it's enough to give Nina goose bumps and make her pleasure wet. She starts to think of where else Ana can touch her body that will yield the same, if not a more powerful reaction.

Nina smiles her charismatic smile at Ana, "I'm here to love you."

Nina knows she can get away with saying almost anything to her in this state. "There was something between us when you almost knocked me and my friend down the other day. I just want to get to know you a bit more."

Ana is struggling at the moment. She is drawn to this woman, for no particular reason other than the essence she has emoting from her being, this feeling like drawing a moth to a flame. A feeling she doesn't want to ignore. Ana knows that this particular woman is off limits because at some point she might just become a part of their investigation to find Nina. She is feeling so conflicted, and dizzy. She gets up from the table and stumbles a bit.

"Oh my goodness... are you okay?" she asks Ana getting up from the table to help her stand.

"Yeah I'll be fine," Ana says almost defiantly, "I need to go outside and get some air."

"Okay let's go outside."

Nina follows Ana outside the bar into the night. They stand there under the street light for a moment while Ana takes her time breathing in the cold evening air. Ana completely forgot she left her jacket in Greg's car and right now she's freezing. She bounces up and down, never actually leaving her feet, and rubs her hands together trying to get warm. There isn't enough alcohol in her system to keep her warm without a coat.

"Here, let me help you," Nina offers, opening up her arms for Ana to come in for a hug. She's hesitant but doesn't want to go all the way back inside the bar knowing that Wren will be there at any moment. Ana breaks several rules of procedure and ethics, but goes into the honey blonde's arms. Nina wraps her hands around her and begins to move them up and down her body to cause friction.

"Thank you," Ana says shivering.

"No problem, we can all use a hand every now and then. So do you think we can meet up for lunch or something? I think we can have a beautiful friendship," Nina asks. Ana doesn't see the devilish smirk sprawled across her face.

"I think lunch would be okay," Ana hesitates.

"You said that like you're not allowed to have lunch or something," Nina replies with a chuckle.

"It's not that it's just that I got a lot going on with work and my family...It's really hard for me to make time you know?" Ana backs out of the embrace so she can see Nina's face.

"I understand," Nina tells her with a genuine smile. They look at each other for a while, unsure of what to do. Nina flashes back to her bathtub orgasm and wants to feel her lips; she wants to taste them. She leans in and Ana doesn't back away. She kisses her soft the first time. She goes in for another kiss, again Ana doesn't back away. Her lips are luscious and Nina can only imagine what her pleasure must taste like. She kisses Ana deeply, moving her tongue around her mouth slowly; seductively; captivating her innermost fantasy. She can taste the beer she was drinking but that doesn't bother her. In fact, it reminds her of Gabriel. Nina wonders what kind of fetishes Ana may have and if they're any similar to Gabriel choking her. Her tongue continues to swirl around Ana's. But, their kiss is broken up by the sound and vibration of Ana's phone going off. Wren is just now pulling up to the bar.

Nina looks at the car approaching them, and turns away so her face is out of view. She kisses Ana on the cheek and gives her a phone number to call her at so they can set up a lunch date. Ana agrees to call her and watches Nina walk away into the night. Ana is blushing like a school girl as she walks up to get into Wren's car. Wren caught a small glimpse of the woman who was standing with Ana and gets a feeling of déjà vu as if he's met her before.

"Who is that?" he asks Ana after she gets in and puts on her seat belt.

"Just a girl I keep bumping into."

"What do you mean?"

"I met her a few days ago while I was working out in the field, but tonight I was here with Greg getting a drink and she happened to be here too."

"Was she there before or after you got to the bar?"

"After..Why?"

"Don't you find it a bit funny that you bumped into this girl while you're working and then now a few days later?"

"Yeah it's a bit coincidental but I don't wanna be paranoid. Every relationship I develop outside of work or my immediate circle shouldn't have to be screened. I'm going to wing it like normal people do," Ana laughs.

"You guys looked pretty close to only have met a few days ago."

"It was cold outside and she was keeping me warm. Wait a minute, you're not jealous are you?"

"Not at all; I'm just concerned. I care about you and something just seems off about her."

"You don't even know her, you two haven't even met. How are you making those kinds of judgment calls?"

"I'm not…just saying what I saw and how I felt. But anyways, I feel like we should do our dinner date over. I mean our last one was okay but you had so much on your mind you couldn't even enjoy yourself. How about a night this week?"

"I'll see what my schedule is looking like and let you know. But the thing with my sister is still going on, and now my other sister had me in some shit this morning with her husband. That just took it out of me. Are you staying the night?"

"Don't I always?"

Ana smiles. "Okay, let's just go back to my place. Nothing crazy just a regular night in the house."

"I'm fine with that, but you have to leave your gun in the car," he demands.

"Get the fuck out of here with that bullshit," Ana erupts. "I'm not leaving my gun in the car! What if somebody steals the car? Or worse what if someone breaks in and I have to go all the way to my backup safe?"

Wren looks at her with the corner of his mouth turned up, "Stop it Ana, you and I both know that's not gonna happen. Just leave it in the car, I hate waking up with the barrel of a gun pointed at me. If you can't do this for me, I'll just drop you off and go home."

Ana thinks about his terms and finally agrees to leave her gun locked in his glove compartment. She is content with having to go to her backup in case of an emergency. And if he feels more comfortable with it in the car, then she will do what she can to make him more comfortable. They get to her house and soon their conversation ends. They cuddle up in her bed to watch late night television until they are both asleep.

Chapter 9

Wren turns over to see Ana still fast asleep. Her crimson curls are everywhere, her mouth is open, and one of her legs is hanging over the side of the bed. A hand is draped across her forehead and the other is nestled inside her panties. He shakes his head at the beauty laying next to him. He peeks under the blanket staring at his manhood fully erect. Instead of poking her in the side to wake her up for some morning sex, he decides to let her sleep for a bit and go drain it in the bathroom. When he comes out of the bathroom, Ana is awake sitting up in the bed looking a bit disoriented.

"Ana, are you okay?" he asks her in a very low tone.

She looks side to side and then to him, "Are we at my house or your house?"

"We're at your house Ana; we always come to your house."

"What did you do with my gun?" she asks, feeling around under her pillow.

"You agreed to leave it locked in my glove compartment. With everything going on with you, I didn't want to chance any accidents with you pulling it on me this morning."

She rolls her eyes. Ana's still in a daze as she looks around for her cell phone. Somehow it ended up underneath the sheets as she retrieves it from near her leg. She looks at the notifications and for once, Anna Lee has not called her a million times or left her any voicemails. She thinks back to the conversation they had with Jason yesterday wondering if that's the cause for her lack of communication this morning. She's sitting with her legs folded underneath her; hunching over as she continues to scroll through her phone.

Wren sits down on the bed next to Ana. He runs his fingers through her hair making her smile and rests her head on his shoulder. He takes this moment to reassure her that he's there if she needs him and everything is going to be okay, eventually. She looks at him lovingly, but in the back of her mind, completely disregards his assistance. Ana assumes that since he doesn't carry a badge there isn't anything that he can do for her situation. They spend the rest of the morning together, just enjoying each other's company before heading out for the day.

After Wren showers and leaves, Ana's first move of the day is to text Eva and schedule a time for them to have lunch:

Hey Eva, it's Ana. I got a day off, you free for lunch around noon?

Nina doesn't waste any time replying back:

Of course I'm free for you, just text me where you wanna meet.

Her response makes Ana blush and smile. She wants to eat at Tommy Jay's but knows that too many people eat there on any given day. She doesn't want to risk anyone seeing them out and about, and it getting back to Greg. She feels like nothing is wrong with her developing a friendship with Eva. The only conflict is Greg following Jeremy around and Eva being so close to him. Since no one can prove her association to Nina, Jeremy or their case she wants to see where things lead. For once, Ana wants to see where her emotions take her. So she messages Eva back the location of a small Spanish restaurant, where they can sit and eat in peace.

A few hours later, Ana is sitting, waiting for the honey blonde to meet her. She finally shows up about fifteen minutes after Ana got there.

"You're late," Ana states very dryly before Nina can even take a seat.

"I apologize," Nina spits out, shifting her gaze from the table to the floor.

"You may sit, but one thing you should know about me is that I don't waste anyone else's time. So you being late to anything we agree upon is wasting time... my time."

"I understand," Nina submits. Ana's statement on time instantly reminds her of Gabriel, but she purposely returns to the mousy demeanor she used around Benjamin. She thinks of Ana as someone sweet, an obstacle, but sweet nonetheless. She felt the same way about Benjamin but killed him without a second thought. She knows that eventually everything is going to come out, and hopefully she won't have to put Ana down. She just hopes Ana moves along with her plans with little resistance. She sits across from her, smiles shyly and looks down at the menu.

Ana doesn't know what to think of this beautiful woman before her. They order their food, and a few drinks while exchanging the normal "getting to know you" banter. Nina tests Ana by asking her what she does for a living. She wants to see if Ana is going to lie to her, but to Nina's surprise she doesn't. The waitress brings over some cocktails and appetizers. Ana tells her she's a federal agent, and because of the case she's working on she won't say anything more than that. Nina asks if it's about Jeremy and if that's the reason why she bumped into them. She says that she was looking into him but he's not a suspect or anything. She just wanted to get a closer look at him, and bumped into her by accident.

Ana decides to change the subject from her job, "So what do you do, Eva?"

"I'm a travel coordinator," Nina answers without missing a beat.

"Really? A travel agent? Those still exist?" Ana questions with a laugh. Ana's phone vibrates in her pocket, but she ignores it.

Nina takes offense even though she's lying about being a travel agent. She rolls her eyes at Ana, "Yes they do. I cater to a very secular group of clients. I personally scout destinations for activities, food and where they will stay. I love to give all of my clients a firsthand experience, a very personal touch. I actually just came back from Russia, and my client loved it so much, he decided he's never coming back."

In that brief moment, she reminisces about Xavier. He allowed Nina to make their plans, and she made sure he's never coming back. She remembers how the blade felt slicing into his flesh, repeatedly, over and over again. Shaking the murderous thoughts from her head she continues to talk about her fake career. "I provide a service that no internet website can. I have the human touch and can plan for both business and pleasure. I ensure experiences my clients will never…

ever…forget."

Ana blushes a little at that last statement, "I apologize, I didn't mean to offend you. But that sounds wonderful; like a very wonderful career. So what about family?"

"What about family?" Nina asks not really wanting to discuss the subject. Her adoptive parents, the Slades, are absolutely loving and caring people. She's already made up her mind to do her best not to involve them in this rampage of chaos she's been on since she started looking for Blake. She can only imagine what they must be going through seeing the story and hearing the police describe her as some kind of monster. She hopes that Jeremy has been checking in on them like she told him to. He's supposed to bring them money at least once a month, and the day he comes bearing flowers they know she's either dead or caught. It makes her a bit sad to think of them, but she chooses to hide her emotions from Ana.

"Do you have a big one, small one?" Ana asks her breaking her from her thoughts. Her phone vibrates in her pocket again. She looks at it, but doesn't recognize the number so she lets it go to her voicemail. She looks up at Nina apologetically, and waits for the answer to her question.

Nina lies, "I'm an orphan. I just bounced around from home to home until I aged out of the system. I got a few scholarships to get myself

through school and worked my ass off to get where I am right now."
Nina is selling this alter ego so well to herself, she's starting to believe
she can actually be Eva Sloane and just erase herself as Nina Slade. She
looks over at Ana, who has a look of pity and admiration. She can tell
that Ana isn't sure if she should trust her or not, but knows that Ana
can't resist her magnetism. Ana's phone vibrates again. This time she
excuses herself from the table and answers the call from the unknown
number.

A few minutes later, Ana comes rushing back to the table a bit
flustered.

"Hey what's going on?" Nina asks feigning concern.

"My sister is hurt and I gotta get down to Metro Hospital right now,"
Ana blurts out. She stumbles a bit and Nina moves out of her seat to
help steady her.

"Maybe I should drive you, seems like those drinks got to you a bit,"
Nina offers.

"Okay maybe you're right," Ana agrees.

Nina takes Ana's car keys from her and they leave the restaurant.
They hop into Ana's Kia and take off toward the hospital. On the way,
Ana dials her sister Lee to let her know what's going on. Anna Lee asks
her if she should come down, but if she does she would have to bring

Bella with her since Jason isn't home. Ana tells her to stay home, so Bella doesn't have to see the chaos going on. She promises to call her back as soon as she gets more information.

Once Nina pulls up to the hospital entrance, Ana barely waits for her to stop the car before hopping out and running inside.

Ana runs up to the information desk flashing her badge and demanding answers. The woman behind the desk is almost as frantic as Ana as she searches through her computer for the information she needs. She finally locates the room Anastasia was checked into, gives her a visitor's pass, and sends her to the elevators.

Ana takes the ride in the elevators up to the fourteenth floor, pacing in small circles and making the other passengers nervous. The elevator finally gets to Asia's floor and Ana sprints through the doors. She stops a nurse along the way to confirm which direction her sister's room was in. She keeps moving until she finally reaches her destination.

There's an officer sitting outside of Anastasia's room, reading a newspaper, and an off-putting man walks up to Ana. He's really young and dressed in an oversized suit. His blonde hair looks like he just rolled out of bed and he stinks of cigarettes. He immediately greets Ana, "Hi I'm Tommy Collins, Anastasia Strayer's attorney." He extends his hand, Ana shakes it with a distasteful look, a bit confused.

"Who the hell are you? I called Chucky to do this pro bono for me."

"Mr. Bateman is extremely busy and knows that you needed this so he told me to handle it for him. No worries though, I have enough experience and your sister is in good hands," the lawyer answers, trying to calm her concerns.

Ana shakes her head looking around at the hospital walls, "Well, what the hell is going on with my sister? And why is that cop sitting there?"

"I'm sorry who are you again?" the cop speaks up.

"I'm Anabelle Strayer, United States Marshal Service! That's my sister in there and I want to know what the FUCK is going on!"

"Please Miss Strayer, you know your sister has a drug problem, right?" the lawyer asks her.

"Of course I do! Anybody who gets within a hundred feet of her knows that! What does that have to do with this?"

"Well, while in lockup, there aren't any drugs readily available—"

"Yeah because it's contraband! They're illegal outside of jail walls and inside jail walls," the cop interrupts from his chair.

Tommy raises his hand in the air to silence the officer. The cop shrugs his shoulders and goes back to reading his newspaper. Tommy turns back to Ana, "Anastasia was going through withdrawal and needed a hit so she sought out drugs within the facility. When she finally scored some, she took it and overdosed. She began to convulse and hit her head on the floor. She's been unconscious ever since."

"What the fuck? How did this happen? These assholes knew she was an addict before she went in! Who was watching her? Isn't she supposed to be under some kind of medical supervision?"

"Actually no," a voice says from behind them. The arresting officer approaches Ana and Tommy, with the Assistant District Attorney by his side. He speaks again, "Strayer! I thought I told you before you can't save her. You don't need to be here complicating things."

"Oh I'm complicating things?" Her voice starts to elevate, "You mean to tell me that I, my sister's emergency contact, don't have the right to be here after one of you buffoons let her OD on some unknown narcotic in your facility. You gotta be FUCKING KIDDING ME! You're lucky I don't have you and your undercover brought up on charges!"

"Oh please," the officer thinks she's speaking of charges in regards to the incident they're all here about, "Charges for what?"

"How about improper behavior of an officer, coercion of a suspect without the presence of council, and sexual assault," that last charge causes a slight shift in the officer's body language that Ana pounces on, "Yeah I see you! You sick bastard! I got your CI, now tell ME who I CAN'T fucking save!"

"Wait! What are you talking about Strayer?" the ADA asks her with a puzzled look on his face. The ADA immediately turns to the officer with a questioning glare trying to figure out what Ana's talking about and if it will actually jeopardize their case.

"At this point it doesn't matter! We're all supposed to be officers of the law and you assholes are breaking and bending it for crack head pussy! You make me sick! Both of you can go fuck yourselves!"

Ana walks away with the attorney to go check in on her sister. Ana doesn't care what happens with them at this point. She just wants to go in to see her sister. They both walk into the room where Anastasia is still out cold. There is a fresh wound on her head that the doctors stapled shut. That must be where she hit her head while she was convulsing. She has tubes pumping fluids into her and a breathing tube down her throat. Seeing her like this is worse than seeing her in the interrogation room all alone.

She leans down and rests her head on her sister's shoulder. She lets a few tears fall. "I'm so sorry Sissy. I should have done more to get you out of this mess. I'm so sorry Sissy. I'm gonna make sure you get out of this. I just wanted you to take some responsibility for yourself for once, but I didn't mean for this to happen. You need a new start. I'll help you Sissy, I promise."

"I think we should go," the attorney speaks up intruding upon Ana's emotional apologies, "She isn't waking up any time soon."

"Okay, so what are those assholes doing out there?" she asks the attorney.

"Well we were supposed to meet at the facility to discuss making a deal for your sister, but you have some information that may get her off and indict the officers on the case?" he questions her accusation from a few moments ago.

"Kind of but there isn't any evidence, it's all hearsay. I just wanted that asshole to know that I knew, and he won't get away with treating my sister like some piece of street trash."

"I get it, I understand, but let me deal with them and I'm pretty sure, U.S. Marshal Strayer, you have work to do," he calmly suggests.

Ana smiles and nods her head. She suddenly remembers that she left Eva downstairs in the car. She thanks the attorney for being there and for calling her. She tells him to make sure he keeps her updated on her sister's condition and her case. As she walks out of the room and toward the elevator, the ADA and arresting officer try to stop her so they can talk but she brushes by them; flipping her middle finger at them both on her way to the exit.

Nina has been sitting in Ana's car for a while. She found a parking space not too far from the hospital and has been on the phone with Jeremy for the last few minutes.

"So you're in the Marshal's car right now?" Jeremy asks in complete shock.

"Yeah we had lunch at some little Spanish dive but then she got an emergency call about one of her sisters. She was a little tipsy at lunch so I volunteered to drive and she actually said yes. I can't believe she trusts me so easily."

"Maybe it was just the fact that she needed to get to her sister safely," Jeremy reasons.

"Who cares why?! All I know is that I'm getting in closer and closer. I can't wait until she finally realizes who I actually am," Nina exclaims with giddiness.

"You sound way too excited about that! I think she's going to kill you when she does," Jeremy says with all the seriousness he could muster, "Seriously...she's going to pull out her gun and shoot you. She's not taking you to jail. Do not pass go; do not collect two hundred dollars."

"Oh my Jer-Bear you worry way too much," Nina tells him.

"Jer-Bear?" He looks at his phone crazily. She never uses nicknames with him. He thinks she's starting to lose her mind a bit. "Listen, I don't know what the hell happened to you out in motherfucking Russia but I need the old Nina back and ready to get shit done! Get it together and get focused. Finish up whatever it is you're doing with clumsy curls so we can get the fuck out of here! There doesn't have to be some big reveal, we just need her and her partner distracted enough for us to leave."

"Okay, okay, Jeremy," she agrees with him just to end his lecture. Nina knows that she doesn't have to do this, but she wants to. She can't wait to reveal to Ana exactly who she is and what she's been up to. She can't wait to Ana's face when she realizes that she has been the one they've been after. She can't wait to see Ana's face when she realizes she's been talking with the enemy, kissing on the enemy, and soon enough sleeping with the enemy. Nina's smile is devilish as she thinks of the evil deeds she has planned for her new "friend".

TAP! TAP! TAP! TAP! The knocking on the window jolts Nina out of her thoughts. She looks across to the passenger side window expecting a meter maid to be there telling her to move the car, but it's Ana. Nina unlocks the door allowing Ana to get into the car. She is noticeably irritated and sober.

"Is everything going to be okay?" Nina asks her feigning concern.

"Huh?" Ana is in a daze, her mind still with her sister.

"With your sister? Is she going to be okay?"

"Oh yeah...I don't know. She has a drug problem, scored some bad ones while she was in lockup and OD'd. I'm sorry this is too much information to start dumping all over you. Thank you for driving me. I just wasn't in a good state of mind to get down here safely. I apologize for taking up so much of your time and I really want to make it up to you Eva," Ana says sincerely.

"Don't worry about it. I'm sure that if I were in a similar situation you would do the same," Nina tries to comfort her.

"I don't know what you're doing or what your plans are for the rest of the day but I could really use a drink. You want to come with me to grab one?" Ana just throws it out there hoping that she can spend some more time with Eva.

"Uuumm, actually I don't have any plans and would love to spend some more time with you. But instead of hitting a bar why don't we go to one of my favorite places and have kind of a spa day. It'll be my treat. You need to relax, get a massage and indulge in yourself for a bit. How does that sound?"

"It sounds expensive and I don't want you to go out of your way to do anything like that for me," Ana tries to decline her invitation.

"I said it's my treat not that I had to pay for it, and besides you NEED this way more than you need any alcohol Ana. Let me do this for you and I promise no more lavish gifts or doting affection. I'll even give you the massage myself to cheapen the experience for you."

They both laugh at her little joke. Ana sighs an exhausted sigh and finally agrees to the pampering.

She just sits back in the seat and allows her new friend to drive her away from the hospital and away from her sister. Thoughts of Anna Lee begin to flash through her mind. She shoots her a quick text message letting her know about their sister's condition. She tells her that she will call her later to update her on everything that went on, but when she has the time she should go down to see her. The hospital isn't going to release her until she wakes up. She continues to go through her phone; responding to messages from Greg and Wren. Finally, Ana decides to put her phone down. It's still her day off and she wants to enjoy the rest of it with this beautiful honey blonde.

They arrive to a small day spa. Nina walks in ahead of Ana to make sure the woman at the desk refers to her as Eva. The woman shrugs her shoulders in an "I can care less" manner and expression. The woman at the desk never questions any of Jeremy's weird friends. They pay her good money to use her spa so she does as she's told.

Ana walks in a few moments later and immediately feels tranquil in the space. She breathes in the aroma therapy candles and lets the ambiance take over her senses. She doesn't even acknowledge the woman at the desk but instead follows Nina right into one of the back rooms.

"Is this place always so empty?" Ana asks.

"It is most of the time. One of my clients owns the place and lets me use it whenever I feel like it. It's a private spa, not open to the public," Nina continues to lie about herself by enlarging the world and life of Eva Sloane. She starts taking off her shirt and undoing her pants.

Ana gets anxious and puts up her hands while shaking them in opposition, "Whoa, whoa! Wait a minute! What's going on?"

Nina laughs at her nervousness. She opens up a locker and takes out two full length white robes. She tells Ana to get undressed and put it on. Ana shakes her head laughing at her initial reaction.

"So clearly... I've never been to a spa before," Ana chuckles pointing fun at herself.

"Yes," Nina giggles, "you've made that real clear. But you can't get a proper massage with clothes on. Now drop them!"

Ana does as she's told.

Chapter 10

Ana is face down on a massage table while Eva prepares a small tray of oils and lotions. Ana is allowing herself to finally relax letting the soft music in the background lull her into a sense of peace and tranquility. Yet, her Zen feeling is immediately disrupted once her phone begins ringing incessantly. She looks down at the device, praying that it wasn't from either of her sisters. She looks at the screen with a twinge of disappointment and answers the call.

"Hey Wren. What's up?" Ana tries to get straight to the point of the call. Nina's ears perk up when she hears Ana answer the phone and say his name. Even though Nina can only hear Ana's side of the conversation; she feels slighted because Ana isn't devoting one hundred percent of her attention to her.

Nina taps her on the leg lightly, "Which one would you like sweetie?" she speaks loud enough for the man on the other end of the line to hear. Ana props herself up on her elbows to turn her head around and face Nina. She motions with her hand to quiet down a bit, and then points to the bottle of lotion in Nina's right hand.

"A friend but does that matter?" Ana asks. "I've already been through a lot today dealing with my sister—No no no she's gonna be fine—I'm okay, I'm just trying to enjoy the rest of this day off. Dinner? Umm—No I do it's just tha—can I just give you a call when I get back ho— No but—It's not that I don't I just don't kn— Will you let me finish a *fucking* sentence?—Fine whatever I'll talk to you later."

Ana hangs up the phone, puts her face back through the hole in the massage table after tossing her phone onto her robe that's sitting on the floor.

Nina smiles at their little spat deciding to use it to her advantage. She rubs some soft smelling lotion between her fingertips and begins to lightly massage Ana on the back of her neck right beneath her ears. Ana moans with satisfaction.

"You're so tense," Nina says to her pushing her fingers deeper into her muscles.

"Uh, I know," Ana moans again, "I really needed this. Thank you."

"Don't worry about it. You know, as friends, we're supposed to make each other's lives a little bit easier. You know, help each other be stress free," she states taking a jab at her conversation with Wren.

Ana laughs catching the subtle dig, "Yeah, I wish all of my friends could understand that."

Nina moves from her neck, down to her shoulders. "Yeah but I understand wanting to spend time with you, too. It's okay to want to be around you more, you're a wonderful person...at least from what I've seen."

Ana falls right into Nina's trap as she relaxes under her touch and begins to open up, "Thank you. I understand that he wants to spend more time with me; it's just that his attitude sucked. And questioning me like that? Who the hell does he think he is?"

"Well are you talking about the guy who came to get you that night we kissed?"

"Yeah," Ana confirms with her cheeks blushing. "He must have heard you and started asking me who was I with? And what was I doing? And then about dinner. He almost sounded a bit jealous."

"Well most boyfriends get jealous when their ladies are out and being secretive about who they're out with."

"I wasn't being secretive," Ana responds defensively, "It's just that he's not even my boyfriend. We don't really interact outside of him coming to pick me up from a bar somewhere. He has no right to be jealous. He has no right to ask me twenty fucking questions about who I'm with, and how I'm spending MY DAY OFF!"

"I'm sorry, I didn't mean to reignite that irritation," Nina apologizes, but a smirk is sprawled across her face. She moves her hands from her shoulders down to her lower back, right above the towel which covers her naked pleasure.

"No it's fine, he 'reignited my irritation!' I just wished he didn't care so much! It would make dealing with him so much easier."

"I get it. Do you think his feelings are about you in general or just about who you're with?" Nina asks still rubbing her to keep her relaxed.

"I don't even know honestly," Ana feels Nina move the towel to start rubbing her derrière. Her heart begins to race as she feels herself getting aroused. Her pleasure is getting wet with anticipation but she's confused because Eva hasn't done anything. But, she wants her to.

"Well do you think he would care if you're with me?"

"I don't know, I guess not. You're no threat to him, I mean it's not like he's going anywhere. He's always gonna be there for me," Ana states without considering how the statement would make her feel.

Nina is no longer smiling. If Ana only knew who she truly was, she would reconsider those words, *You're no threat to him.* Nina inhales deeply to calm herself down, and decides to test the validity of what Ana just said. She wipes the lotion on her fingers off with a wet towel. She takes two of her wet fingers and lightly rubs the line that seems to be keeping her pleasure shut. She waits for Ana to protest, or to flinch, but she doesn't do anything. She's letting her have her way with her on this massage table. So Nina continues. She moves her fingers back over the line and this time she parts her lips to truly feel the softness of her womanhood. Ana relaxes into the sensation traveling through her body. She gets wetter. Nina is reminded of Gabriel, and how wet he made her and is instantly turned on. She moves her fingers inside of her quickly without hesitation. Ana cries out in ecstasy while gripping the massage table trying to prevent herself from stopping Eva. Nina continues to move her fingers in and out of her walls until she climaxes.

Ana exhales unable to believe the orgasm she just had at the hands of this beautiful woman. She turns over to look at the honey blonde woman moving around the room. She watches her grab a pillow and then come up to the head of the table where she's now on her back but propped up on her elbows. Nina motions for her to sit all the way up. She hits a lever somewhere on the table that brings it to a slightly upright position. She places a pillow behind her and tells her to lean back and move forward. Ana does as she's told. Nina walks back to the end of the table and grabs a small stool to sit on.

The first thing Ana feels is Eva grabbing her under her thighs and moving her closer to the edge of the table resting her legs onto her shoulders. The next feeling of euphoria comes with the moist tip of Nina's tongue sliding slowly between Ana's lips. Ana arches her back completely enveloped in bliss. Ana doesn't know what to do. She squirms around, but Nina holds her firmly in place ensuring that she can't get away from her tongue. The pleasure is almost too much to bear. She wriggles around gripping the table as Nina's magnificent mouth muscle moves over her most intimate parts. She can barely contain the sounds escaping her with every breath, with every lick, with every supple kiss. She climaxes again and again.

Nina finally stops her verbal assault on Ana's labia and stands up from her stool. She walks up to where her head is laying on the pillow, the glow of her orgasms glistening off of her skin, and leans down kissing her gently on the lips. Ana can taste her own juices; she can smell her very essence wafting from Nina's mouth. Ana sits straight up suddenly panicking about everything that has just happened.

"I can't believe this! This was a mistake!" Ana swings her legs off of the table to the floor. She starts looking around for her robe. She bends down to pick it up off of the floor. When she puts it on, Nina is standing there in front of her. She grabs her shoulders lightly and looks Ana right into her big blue eyes.

"It's okay that you feel this way," Nina speaks softly while stroking the side of her face with the back of her hand, "Today was something special. It was just for you to relax and get away from everything… even if just for a moment. I know that whatever is happening with your sister can't be easy to deal with, and your job must be even harder so I know that you needed this. It doesn't have to happen again. I'm just glad you let today happen."

"I don't know what to say," Ana is in shock, "You get it. I've never had anyone just…get…it." Her thoughts automatically drift to Wren. Although, he wasn't very understanding over the phone she knows how much he cares and it's not fair to him that she's been treating him the way she has.

"Are you going to be okay?" Nina asks breaking into her thoughts.

"I'm going to be fine, thank you," Ana looks at the blonde beauty with eyes full of sincerity, "Seriously, thank you. Today was like nothing I've ever experienced before and I loved every minute of it. But I just have too much going on and I don't want to get caught up—"

Nina stops her from rambling on by holding her hand. The gesture is so gentle and sympathetic.

Ana just looks at her as if she is too good for her. She shakes her head, almost on the verge of tears, "I have to go. Are you okay getting home from here?" Ana can't fathom taking Eva anywhere at this moment. She doesn't want to even consider what that car ride conversation would be like. She looks at Eva apologetically before dashing out of the room to get her things. Today's antics went too far. Her constant swapping of lovers had calmed down since she met Wren...it had actually stopped altogether. Today, however, she crossed a line, both personally and professionally. She hops in her car and drives straight home. All she wants to do is be alone for a minute to get her head together. She needs to refocus on her job and stop allowing these distractions to divert her.

She finally makes it to her house and immediately recognizes that something's wrong. Wren is sitting in his car; waiting in front of her house. But, what makes her even more nervous is her sister's car is parked in front of his. She pulls into her driveway and walks the pathway to her front door. Wren gets out of his car and walks up next to her. Ana looks past him at her sister's car, but Anna Lee isn't in it. She must be inside already. She looks back at Wren.

"Now isn't a good time. I don't want to clean up our conversation from earlier, and I'm not interested in dinner tonight. I'll call you in the morning," Ana starts firing off before he can even say anything.

"I know tonight isn't a good night for you, I just came by to apologize. I was frustrated earlier and I didn't mean to take it out on you." He grabs her by the hand. His touch is warm, but his hands are rough. It gives her chills and makes her smile knowing that he still cares for her so much.

"You didn't need to come all the way here. You could have called," Ana tells him in a sweet tone.

"I tried calling but your phone isn't on. It kept going straight to voicemail, and I couldn't leave things the way they were."

Ana looks at him confused while reaching into her pocket for her phone. She pulls it out and powers it back on. She doesn't remember turning it off. *Maybe Eva did,* she thinks to herself, "but why?" She shakes the thought loose from her head, as it seems too ridiculous to be true.

"What? What's the matter?" he asks reading the expression on her face.

"Nothing," she says shaking her head.

Before he can say anything else, Anna Lee opens up the door. Wren and Ana turn to look at her. Anna is noticeably upset. "You need to come inside Sissy. We have to talk," Anna demands. She walks back inside the house leaving the front door open behind her. Wren turns to leave but Ana stops him by grabbing his hand. The motion tells him to follow her inside. She doesn't want to be alone with her sister right now. She knows that something isn't right.

Anna is sitting at the kitchen table with a glass of wine. Ana walks into the house and tells Wren to just sit in the living room until she finds out why her sister has let herself into her house and into her wine cabinet. She sits down across from her sister wondering what the hell is going on.

"What's the matter Sissy?" Ana blurts out anxiously awaiting for her news. "If it's about Jason, and that phone call, I'm done! I already told you I'm done! DO NOT ask me to do anymore recon on him!"

"It's not about Jason, Anabelle," Anna calmly states.

"Well what is it? Why did you let yourself into my house? What's happened? Is it Bella?" Ana's anxiety is growing because Anna called her by her full name.

"No, Bella is fine," Anna Lee inhales deeply, "It's Asia."

"Oh I thought it was gonna be something serious. I was just there earlier today. Relax, she has a lawyer, she's gonna get into rehab and she's gonna be fine."

"Anastasia died two hours ago Anabelle," Anna Lee finally spits it out.

Ana feels like someone just punched her in the gut. The blood rushing to her face makes her hot as her eyes swell with tears. She stands up from her chair at the table turning around slowly as if she's looking for something to throw, but picks up nothing and sits back down. She lets her hair down allowing the crimson curls to fall in front of her face. After a few minutes of awkward fidgeting, Ana finally finds her words again, "How? I was just there, she was asleep; she was going to be okay."

"When I went down to see her I was in the room and a whole bunch of sounds and noises started going off. She started having trouble breathing. The doctor came in and discovered she had an aneurysm in her abdomen. The drug use made her more susceptible to it, but it also compromised her ability to undergo major surgery. They did everything they could to fix the damage, but she was bleeding out too fast. The drugs she took hadn't been fully flushed from her system and it was just too much stress on her body. She didn't make it out of the operating room."

"What the hell Sissy?! Why didn't you call me?"

"I DID!" Anna yells, "That's why I'm here! You weren't answering your phone, so I had to come here and let you know!"

"This doesn't make any sense! She was fine!" Ana starts screaming at her sister as if it will change the news she has just given her. "She was fine! She was fine! I saw her! She was going to be okay!" Wren comes

in as Ana is spiraling. She immediately turns to him and buries her face

into his chest. All he can do is stand there in silence holding her; rubbing

her back as she cries.

Wren can barely keep himself from crying. He looks to Anna Lee

who is in a weird space. She's gripping her wine glass with both hands

just staring into the burgundy liquid. The sobs of her sister finally break

into her thoughts forcing Anna Lee to let her tears flow. They remain

in that moment for a while. No one speaks, no one leaves; they stay in

that moment acknowledging and dealing with the unexpected loss of

Anastasia.

***

The following morning is surprisingly bright and sunny as Ana wakes

up. She doesn't remember falling asleep. She just wants to remember

yesterday as a nightmare that she's now waking up from. She's hoping

that the news Lee told her was wrong; that she just imagined it but she

is still in the same clothes from yesterday. Wren is still sleeping in her

bed. She walks downstairs to put some coffee on, but her sister already

beat her to it. Ana steps into the aroma circulating her kitchen. Anna

Lee is walking around getting things together to finish making breakfast

and talking away on her phone. She sounds like she's talking to Jason

about Bella, so Ana just maneuvers her way around her sister to make herself a cup of coffee. Ana looks at her sister move around as if nothing is wrong.

Ana sits down at the kitchen table lost in her thoughts until her sister slides a plate of food in front of her and runs her fingers through those crimson curls before going back to cooking. "You need to eat Sissy," Lee orders her oldest sister.

"I'm not hungry, the coffee will be fine," Ana refuses, pushing the plate away. Anna Lee is not going to accept no for an answer. She stops what she's doing, turns around and sits down at the table. She pushes the food back toward her sister, demanding that she eat.

"You need to eat Anabelle! I have too much to take care of without worrying if you're eating or not." She goes into full mom mode. Ana caves in quickly deciding to take a few bites and avoid getting into an argument with her. Her behavior reminds her of their mother.

"Wait. Does Mom know Sissy?"

"Of course she does!" Lee answers, "But she doesn't want to see anyone. She doesn't want to be bothered. I'm going over there today after I get myself home and showered. I'm going to take Bella since that will help keep her spirits up. She explicitly said that no one should be sad. Before her demons took over, Asia was full of love and life and that's how she wants us to be."

Ana rolls her eyes. She knew who Asia was. She knew the kind of troubled woman she was; even before her demons took over. But Ana knows that their mother and her baby sister were always in denial about Asia. The only help they believed she needed was Anabelle keeping her out of jail. A sudden rush of guilt floods her and she struggles to hold back her tears.

"It's not your fault Sissy," Anna Lee seems to know what she's thinking. She holds her sister's hands. Ana inhales deeply, wipes her eyes in her shirt and gets up from the table. She empties her plate and puts it in the sink. She walks up behind her sister, who's still sitting at the table and kisses her on the top of her head.

"Thank you Sissy for being here. Do you need any help with the arrangements or with Mom?"

"No Sissy, I know you still have a case to work—"

"Are you fucking kidding me? I can't go to work now! I'll get somebody else to cover or something. I'll figure it out."

"No, this is your first case back in the field, you need it right now. You don't need any reason for them to doubt you're ready. You let them know what's going on, you take a day off for the service, but you keep working and show them how much of a badass you really are!"

Wren comes down at the tail end of her pep talk. Ana turns to look at him and then at her sister. They both instantly burst into laughter.

Anna Lee blushes, "It was too much, right?" She joins in their laughter.

"Yeah Sissy, a bit much. But I get it. I know what you mean, and I'll do it," Ana agrees as their giggles die down.

"So does that mean I'm driving you to work this morning?" Wren interjects into the conversation.

"Yeah I'll go in today and let them know what's going on," Ana states walking past Wren. She goes upstairs to get ready for work; leaving Wren and Anna Lee in the kitchen alone. Wren makes himself a cup of coffee and sits down at the table. He looks at Anna Lee but doesn't speak. She's not in a conversational mood either.

She gets up from the table and makes him a plate of food. She slides it in front of him to which he thanks her quietly. She nods her head with a smile and returns to the stove to start cleaning up the kitchen.

Normally, this moment would be her opportunity to bombard her sister's lover about where their relationship is headed and what are his plans for the future. However, her mind has already entered into planner mode. She gets back on her phone to finish making arrangements for her sister's funeral.

Ana comes down the stairs fully showered in a pair of dark denim jeans and a U.S. Marshal cotton tee shirt. She grabs her vest from the front closet, along with her holster and duffle bag. Her hair is pulled up into a tight bun. There isn't a curly tendril out of place. She has the tiniest bit of makeup under her eyes to hide the puffiness, but she is effortlessly beautiful. Wren looks at her as he puts his jacket on. He is infatuated with her. He watches her as Ana moves around her living space going over her mental checklist for everything she needs to get through her day. She finally goes into the kitchen, kisses her sister on the cheek and runs out the door to Wren who is now waiting inside of his car.

"You know I could have taken myself to work," she says with a smile.

"I know but now you need to call me to come get you when you get off. And I mean that in the most non-stalkerish type of way," he chuckles. She laughs at him shaking her head.

"You know I don't have to call you. There are other people I can call. Not to mention my partner who doesn't have any problems giving me a ride anywhere," she counters.

"Oh I know, but call me anyway. I want to make sure you're okay," he reasons with her in a softer tone. They pull up to her office and he looks at her before she reaches for the handle to get out of the car, "Listen to me...Today isn't going to be easy but I'm gonna be around if you need me for anything. I don't care what it is. I'm here for you."

"Why are you so wonderful?" she asks him rhetorically.

"Because I've done unimaginable things in my life and being here with you is a chance for me to be someone I never was. Go to work; I'll be here to pick you up later," he orders. He doesn't give her any time to debate, and Ana doesn't want to. She wasn't expecting him to answer her the way that he did. It made her curious as to who Wren really is. What could he have possibly done in his life that was so unimaginable? All Ana knows is that the man driving her around, her designated dick is a complicated one who is so caring and concerned for her. She can feel how much he cares; she can see it in his eyes. Suddenly another rush of guilt comes over her. She thinks about Eva and their day together. She makes up her mind that now isn't the time for new friends and she knows that she needs to distance herself from her; especially if she wants to see where things go with Wren. Asia passing away is beginning to put things in perspective for her and she's finally starting to see what she wants in her life.

Chapter 11

Greg's feet are propped up on the wall forcing him to lean back in one of Ana's office chairs while Ana sits behind her desk. He tosses a stress ball to her and waits for her to toss it back as they contemplate what their next move should be. They ran through all of the leads from Detective Flynn's notes and have hit a brick wall. Greg looks to Ana, wondering how she's handling everything. Almost as if she can read his mind she tells him, "I'm fine! Don't worry so much." She never stops tossing the ball.

"Are you sure?" he catches the ball, doubting her calmness, "I mean I know how much Asia meant to you. Are you sure you're okay?" He tosses it back to her.

"Yes I'm fine," she catches the ball, "Everyone deals with grief in their own way. I've been at my mom's house with Anna and she's in Captain Commando mode, my mom is giving me the silent treatment, and I just got tired of being there. I need to be here focused on work. We need this case to end so we can move on to the next one."

"Yeah about that," Greg turns around stopping their game of catch. He looks at his partner of five years with a smile and suddenly loses his train of thought.

"Greg!" Ana yells snapping her fingers in front of his face, "About what?"

"Umm nothing...never mind," Greg remembers what he wants to say but chickens out.

"Don't never mind me dipshit! You say what you gotta say! I got enough going on in my life right now without having to worry about whether or not my partner is keeping secrets from me! So spit it out!"

"Fine, after this case I won't be your partner anymore," Greg lets the words fall from his mouth. Ana is speechless. She wants to believe that he's joking, but his tone and the look in his eyes says he is not. She continues to stare at him in silence waiting for an explanation. He finally gives in to those big blue eyes that are burning a hole into the side of his face. He can't even look at her as he speaks, "It's been a while we been doing this, and I'm tired. Ripping and running all over the city, sometimes all over the country...it gets exhausting. So I've been looking at some desk jobs and a few promotions so I can have straight hours and less action."

"Is this what you want? Or is this what Sharron wants?"

"Don't do that! You know she has very little to do with the decisions I make for my career. Besides I actually enjoy being with my wife. Despite whatever you think; I actually enjoy being married and playing with my kids. I don't want to be at work sixteen hours a day and then come home and pass out. I'm missing too much. And regardless if I get one of the promotions I put in for or not, this is going to be my last field case."

"Well maybe you don't have to change positions sort of speak. Maybe you can just be my investigator. You know...do all the tech stuff back here at the office," she suggests hoping to sway his decision. Greg just shrugs his shoulders not wanting to continue the conversation. He gets up from his chair and walks over to her desk. He starts to flip through the case file on her desk. He stops when he reaches the names of Nina's parents. He taps the paper, with a perplexed look on his face and then walks out of Ana's office.

"Hey where are you going? What's wrong?" she shouts after him. He doesn't answer back, but returns to the room with his notepad in hand. He's flipping through the pages incessantly, back and forth, back and forth.

"What the hell is wrong with you?!" Ana asks getting annoyed that he's blatantly disregarding her questions.

"Why haven't we spoken to the Slades?" he finally speaks.

"Huh?"

"Nina's parents! Why haven't we spoken to them yet?! We haven't gone to their house or anything?" His voice is full of surprise.

"I don't know," Ana starts flipping through her notes as well. She's shaking her head in disbelief that the both of them, as seasoned officers, didn't think to question them sooner. She finds their home number and calls it. She gets a cute voicemail from the Slades but decides not to leave a message.

"No one's home," she says looking up at Greg.

"I can't believe we didn't get to them sooner," he says still shaking his head at their huge blunder. "What if she's been hiding out there this entire time?!"

"I'm pretty sure she hasn't. Besides this is my fault anyway. If I hadn't got so caught up in my sister's mess, we could've been more focused on the case. I got way too distracted and it's beginning to interfere with our job...with you." Ana buries her face into her hands.

Greg walks around behind her and rubs her back to soothe her.

"You're right," he begins, moving his hands to her shoulders, "This is all your fucking fault!"

Ana pulls her face out of her hands turning up to look at him. One of his eyebrows is arched high and his mouth is scrunched toward the side of his face. His expression is priceless as they both erupt into laughter. After he catches his breath; he shows his sincerity.

"Listen to me, life happens, shit happens and we all gotta deal with it the best way we know how. Who was supposed to know that this case would land on our desk just as your sister is getting into trouble? And then the result from that is her death? Are you serious Ana? We all have our distractions but the thing here is I didn't catch this either. We both fucked up! Let's just figure out how we can get in touch with them and get back into the chase." He pats her on the back before walking away to his own office.

Ana is so disappointed in herself that she let her sister get in the way of her job. Although she is very much saddened by her sister passing, she knows that it was inevitable. The road her sister chose after their father passed away was rough for her. It was rough on all of the Ana's...Anabelle was only sixteen, Anastasia was thirteen and Anna Lee was only eight when their father lost his life. Ana spins her chair away from her desk to stare out of her office window as memories from that day saunter through her thoughts:

Anabelle was walking home from school. It was a bright and beautiful day. It had been the nicest day they had seen in a while during the rainy spring. Scents of new flowers budding filled the air while the light breeze hugged her gently. She made sure to walk just a little bit slower to enjoy the cool air blowing through her crimson curls. It would be a great day to take her sisters to the park and ride their bikes. Ana just knew that this day was going to be a great day. She inhaled deep, luxuriating in the afternoon sun. Once she finally reached her house, she noticed her dad's work car parked out front. She just knew that this day was meant to be perfect! It was beautiful outside AND her daddy came home from work early! With a smile as wide as can be, she trotted up the walkway and burst into the house. She dropped her bag by the door, tossed her jacket on the coat rack, and began shouting for her father to come sit outside on the porch with her, to finish her homework. She walked past the stairs and into the kitchen where her mother was sitting at the table with two men. She walked closer and spoke to her mother as if the men weren't there. She demanded to know where her father was since his car was parked outside. One of the men, she knew as her dad's partner and the other was the Lieutenant of his squad. Her mother had a blank stare on her face as the two men spoke to her softly, until Ana came into the room asking for her father. Ana's mother finally broke down. Ana had never seen her mother cry and it was one of the most disturbing things she had ever witnessed. All her mother could do was sob uncontrollably. The noise could only be described as a panther in heat. The sound of her mother's wails made her cringe and her own eyes water. The two men stood up to leave them in this dreaded space. Her sisters had not gotten off the school bus yet, and Ana knew she would have to be the one to tell them. She helped her weeping mother up from the table and to the sofa in the living room, where she laid on the cushion and buried her sorrows into the pillows. She left her mother, walking to the front door to let the two men out of their home. When she opened the door the sun shined brightly making her put her hand up to block its beautiful rays. In that moment, ALL sunny days had been ruined for Ana.

Ana is still sitting in her office chair; staring out of the window into the sun-filled afternoon. Thoughts of her father lead to thoughts of her sisters. Anna Lee has been taking care of all the arrangements and she is happy to let her. Ana was the one who organized her father's funeral and vowed to never plan another one. She never expected the next funeral she went to would be one for her little sister. The emotions swirling around in her head sent a tear to her eye. Her reflection in the window appears weak and broken. She shakes the image, wipes away the tear, and stands up out of her chair. Ana turns away from the window just in time for Greg to poke his head in her office with a light tap on the open door.

"I found them," he announces with a beam of excitement. Ana doesn't hesitate grabbing her navy blue jacket with the huge U.S. Marshal insignia on the back. She heads out of her office with Greg. She hates the jacket. She always feels like there's a target literally painted on her back, but it's the only jacket of hers that fits when she has her vest on. They make their way downstairs to the car. Greg lets Ana know that he was able to track the Slades on a cruise in the Caribbean somewhere. She's glad that he knows where the Slades are but is more interested in where *they* are going since the people they're looking for are on a ship in the middle of an ocean. He says they're boarding passes were traded in for plane tickets because Mr. Slade had a bad episode of seasickness and they were coming home. They're going to be landing in two hours at a small airport not too far away. Ana wonders if Nina will be dumb enough to meet her parents at the airport.

Ana and Greg make it to the airport and head straight to the Arrivals Terminal. They stand inside for what seems to be hours waiting for the Slades to come in. They speak with airline security and let them know what flight they're waiting for and to make sure the the Slades are escorted off the plane and directly to them. All Ana can do is pace around the arrival gate in circles. She's making Greg dizzy as he sits in the uncomfortable plastic chair waiting for the flight to land.

"I thought you said they were landing in two hours? We've been here for three," Ana complains to Greg while continuing to pace around the empty gate. She looks at her watch and shakes her head. She is growing more and more impatient as the time passes.

Finally, airline security approaches them and says that there had been a delay when the flight took off which is why it's coming in so late. However, it will be touching down within the next twenty minutes. Security was made aware of a sick passenger on board, it was Mr. Slade. They brought over a wheelchair and had an ambulance waiting outside.

Thankfully for Ana and Greg, the Slades were the first two passengers to get off the plane. Flight crew members help Mr. Slade into the wheelchair and immediately begin to move him to the ambulance. Ana looks around hoping to see if Nina is anywhere in the vicinity but she doesn't see anyone. She turns her focus to Mrs. Slade, who is a tall lean woman with luxurious gray hair flowing down slightly past her shoulders. A few wrinkles around her eyes, but she was stunning for a woman approaching sixty. Her freshly tanned skin is glowing from their days under the Caribbean sun as she moves effortlessly in a long sundress. She is wearing sunglasses, but her face is visibly full of worry for her husband. Mrs. Slade is confused in the commotion, with EMT workers treating her husband, airport security asking her a million questions and Ana flashing her badge in her face and telling her that she needs to come with them.

Mrs. Slade has had enough of the onslaught and raises her hands to silence everyone. Her voice is stern and direct as she begins to answer all of the questions coming to her. She tells security that a full report is available with the flight manifest and she doesn't have time to go through their inquiry again. She asks Ana if she or her husband are under arrest for anything, to which she shakes her head no.

"Well, fine since we are not under arrest and you probably want to know something about our daughter; you can ride with me in the ambulance with my husband. You have until we get to the hospital to get whatever information you need, but after that you assholes are on your own." She walks away from the crowd, following the EMT's to the ambulance.

Ana follows Mrs. Slade and tells Greg to get the car and follow behind the ambulance.

Unfortunately for the Marshals, the ride to the hospital is short. Greg pulls into the emergency bay of the hospital where Ana is standing there waiting for him. Ana gets into the car with a huge sigh. Greg is antsy as he taps his fingers on the steering wheel waiting for Ana to talk.

"So," he looks at his partner, "What did she say?!"

Ana just shrugs her shoulders and shakes her head. "She's delusional."

"What?" Greg's face mimics his question. "What do you mean she's delusional?"

"Exactly what I said! She sat in that ambulance and told me that her daughter had nothing to do with what happened at La Rouge Cosmetics. And when I asked her where Nina was. She said she has no idea. She hasn't spoken to her in months. So I asked her if she was worried about her daughter and she said that she hadn't received any flowers so she knows she's okay. I asked her what that meant. She says that Jeremy comes by every couple of weeks with money and gifts from Nina, and if he delivers them a bouquet of flowers it means that she's either dead or captured. But she knows that Nina is lying low until this thing blows over and that once WE vindicate her through our investigation, she'll come home. But that's all I got from the Slades. Dad doesn't look like he'll be any better to talk to. So I just left her with my business card and if she has anything she needs to tell us to give me a call."

"DAMN IT!!!" Greg slams his fist on the steering wheel, "WHERE THE FUCK IS THIS BITCH?!"

"Easy killer, we'll find her," Ana chuckles at his anger. Greg calms himself and just drives back to the office after yet another dead end.

By the time Ana gets back into her office her phone has several missed calls and incoming texts from Eva. She stares at the device and it rings again. It's Eva … she sends the call straight to voicemail.

She takes off her vest and throws it in her duffel bag, along with her navy blue jacket that she hates. She releases her tight red coils from their bun letting them cascade down her back. She grabs her leather jacket and walks out of the building. She's half way to the parking garage when she remembers the Wren dropped her off this morning. She smiles because he was right, she has to call him to get her from work. Luckily for her, he's already waiting outside.

Wren looks at the red head beauty looking at him sitting in his car. She shakes her head but he can see the smile painted across her face. He can see those big blue eyes coming toward him. Ana walks up to the car, opens the rear passenger door to toss her bag inside, and then gets into the front seat. She leans in and kisses him on the lips. He smiles at her but doesn't speak. He drives away from the building with his crimson curled beauty by his side.

Jeremy and Nina are sitting in Jeremy's car watching as Ana gets into the car with Wren. Nina takes out her cell phone and dials Ana again. Again...her call is sent to voicemail. She is growing increasingly frustrated with Ana. Her face is red with rage, and all Jeremy can do is sit there and watch.

"I just need her to answer the phone! I need to get back in with her! This is ruining EVERYTHING I had planned!"

"Well, what did she say the last time you spoke to her?"

"Her sister was sick in the hospital or something, and then we had our thing at the spa, and after that she said it was too much. She had too much going on and doesn't want to get caught up. I've been sending her countless messages and she's not answering my phone calls. It's just really starting to piss me off!" Nina is letting her anger get the best of her but is distracted when Jeremy's phone rings. He takes the call and it's very brief.

"Well, if that's pissing you off. I don't know how you're going to take this," he cringes back toward the door anticipating a violent reaction from her.

"What? Who was that on the phone?" Nina demands to know.

"It was Momma Slade," he says in a low tone.

"Well? What's going on? What happened?" Nina asks growing worried of whatever news Jeremy is about to tell her.

"Well apparently your folks came back from their trip early. Your dad had a bad case of food poisoning and sea sickness. They got on a flight and were met at the airport by Tweedle Dee and Tweedle Dum. Your girlfriend took the trip in the ambulance with your mother and was asking her questions about you of course. But since your mom doesn't know anything that's going on she couldn't tell them anything. It's not like she believes you did any of this anyway. But anyway she told me that they're keeping your dad overnight and to come pick them up tomorrow afternoon."

"SHE WENT TO SEE MY MOTHER!," Nina starts punching the dashboard, "Ugh…THAT… BITCH!"

Jeremy reaches over in an attempt to stop her from bruising his car but is met with a cold stare of opposition. "Don't touch me!"

He immediately backs off, raising his hands in defeat. He doesn't know what she will do to him in this temperament. All he can do is look at his friend go through her emotions. He watches as Nina calms herself down from an enraged fit to worrisome daughter. The morph is too visual for Jeremy as he soon begins to truly see how deranged Nina is. Nina runs her fingers through her short hair and almost as if pushing the anger out of her, she exhales while moving her palms in a downward motion.

"I hope Daddy is okay," Nina finally says as if she didn't just have an episode in the car.

"Oh honey…are YOU okay?" Jeremy asks with a raised eyebrow.

"I'll be fine. But play time is over. Let's go," she responds cynically.

"Um, where are we going?" Jeremy asks with a twinge of fear in his voice.

"HOME! Let's go home! I'll see that bitch sooner or later and when I do, I'll make sure she doesn't bother my parents ever again! They have nothing to do with this and she's dragging them through an investigation."

"To be fair, they aren't being investigated Nina," Jeremy offers up trying to reason with the murderess.

"Don't!" she holds up her finger, "Just shut up and drive! We'll pick this back up tomorrow morning. Early tomorrow morning. We'll follow these two idiots for a bit more just to see how much my timeline needs to speed up."

Jeremy shakes his head to himself making sure not to say anything else to Nina. Being back here is making her sloppy, and a bit crazy. He thinks she was better off in Russia with Xavier and the mobster trying to sell her pussy out of his garden. All he can do is drive and hope that whatever she's planning doesn't land him in jail.

Chapter 12

The sun is shining brightly as Ana gazes into the leaves of the trees above their heads. The birds are singing and the breeze is flowing gently while the group of mourners step lightly past tombstones and burial plots. The fresh flowers budding sprinkle the air with their delightful aroma. The grass beneath their feet is soft and quiet as they walk to Anastasia's final resting place. Days like today are just another reason for Ana to hate sunny and beautifully perfect days.

Wren has been holding her hand, helping her over the divots in the grass, making sure she doesn't stumble. Ana can only imagine the scene she would cause if she tripped in her white dress at her sister's burial. Ana's dress is white chiffon scattered with cherry blossoms and her curly crimson hair is pulled back into a soft French braid. She's extremely uncomfortable in the dress and shows as such with her constant fidgeting. Wren notices how uncomfortable she is and squeezes her hand just a little bit. It forces Ana to take a deep breath in and exhale to calm herself down. This mundane act of lowering Asia into the ground, while everyone stands around to watch is obscene to Ana. She can't wait until this is over, and she knows Wren feels the same way.

Wren doesn't want to be at a funeral today but knows that he needs to be here for Ana. He wanted to meet her sisters since the day he found out she had them, but today isn't the kind of day introductions need to be made. Ana is the first woman he's been involved with in a very long time. He cares so much for her and never wants to rush her because he knows she's a runner. Today, more than ever, shows that he won't leave her. He'll stand by her side and protect her by any means, but today...watching her sister be laid to rest is one of those things he could not shield her from. He couldn't stop her death. He didn't even see it coming...no one did.

Ana stands next to Wren, resting her head on his shoulder, still hand in hand. She sighs and closes her eyes as some woman, from one of Anna Lee's mommy groups, sings a beautiful rendition of *Silent Night*. It was Asia's favorite Christmas jingle and their mother thought the lyrics were so fitting for the occasion. The woman continues to sing the lyrics, most of which are unknown to Ana. She never learned the words beyond, "Sleep in heavenly peace." A single tear falls from her eye, and suddenly she hears the uncontrollable sobbing that she had only heard once before in her lifetime. It is the dreadful noises of her mother's anguish over losing another piece of her soul. As the casket lowers, the final words of *Silent Night* fill the intimate space of strangers along with the bellows of her mother's tears. It's a cacophony of noise that is no longer suitable for the moment, so Anna Lee's friend finishes the song, and stops singing.

Ana feels a strange force come over her; moving her toward her crying mother. She knows better but she can't help herself. She slips her hand out of Wren's and just seems to float to her mother who is curled over at the waist, still belting those wretched sounds, always reminiscent of a panther in heat, those sounds of her wounded soul. Ana looks at Anna Lee, who has tears streaming down her beautifully made up face but will not utter a sound. Anna Lee is clutching their mother with all of her might trying to ensure that she doesn't fall into the plot with the lowering casket.

Ana mouths to her, "Where's Jason?" To which Lee motions her head toward the crowd behind them. Ana stands up for a moment to see why her brother-in-law left her sister to deal with their mother by herself. Past the edge of the crowd is a single man rocking a sleeping toddler. He's walking back and forth, around in circles, speaking gently into little Bella's ears, rubbing her back. It makes Ana smile until the wails of her mother bring her back to the moment in front of her.

She looks over to Lee, mouthing to her that they should move their mother to the car. Anna Lee agrees with a quick nod and bends down to whisper something into their mother's ear. They both begin to move her, guiding her toward the row of cars lining the edge of the grass.

Mrs. Strayer finally stands upright to assist them in helping her to the car. Ana hands her a handkerchief to dry her face and it is at that moment their mother realizes it is Ana who is on the other side of her. She pulls her shoulder away from Ana, shifting her entire body toward Anna Lee. In a tone only audible to her two daughters she speaks, "You don't touch me! You don't speak to me—"

"Mother!" Anna Lee whispers cutting her off in an attempt to stop whatever onslaught is about to spew from her mouth. She continues to guide her mother and Ana follows so whoever is in earshot cannot hear what is coming either.

"Hush Lee! Anabelle, I am done with you! *Your father*, God rest his soul, had always told you to watch over your sisters. I have always told you to watch over your sisters. Lee has told you to find our Asia and to save her." Her voice is quivering as it begins to crack, "but you sat back and did nothing to save my baby. You did nothing to save my baby. Now you leave me be! You leave me alone! I don't want to see you! She's gone! Anastasia is gone and you didn't save her! You DID NOT save her!" She pushes Ana away from her.

Her mother stood at an even five feet, the years of worrying about Anastasia in the street and Anabelle as an officer had taken its toll on her. Revealing themselves through the many worry lines creasing around her eyes and forehead. She is frail with a head full of soft grey and black hair, and green eyes that can pierce your soul. But the action of her frail hand pushing her away left Ana feeling like she had just been hit by a freight train. The words had knocked the wind out of her and she was no longer floating...she was falling.

Ana's knees buckle, her hand raises to her mouth to muffle the sound of her gasping from the malicious assault of her mother's tongue, and she falls. Without missing a beat, Wren is right there behind her to steady her. She is more surprised that she didn't hit the dirt than at him being there to catch her. His strong arms wrap around her, holding her, saving her. He stands there silently waiting for Ana to tell him what to do.

"Please just take me home," Ana's voice shakes with her request. For the first time, since she knew Anastasia had passed... she cries. She rests her head on Wren's shoulder as he walks her to his car. The tears drip onto his blazer, and although he has no idea what was said, he knows that it shook Ana to her core. He knew from the moment she let go of his hand and went to her mother; she was going to need him.

So he is there for her.

Ana doesn't care what happens, she just wants to leave. She doesn't wait for fellow mourners to bestow their condolences upon her, she doesn't wait for Anastasia to be buried, and she doesn't wait for the crowd to disperse. She allows Wren to walk her to his car, open the front passenger door and help her inside. She sniffles and wipes away her tears while he walks around to the driver's side. He gets into the car. He looks over at his crimson-haired beauty taking her chin into his hand; he kisses her so delicately on the lips. He looks deep into her big blue eyes, "I don't care what was said, but what I do know is that *This!*," he motions to everything around them, "*This! None of this* ... was your fault! Don't you dare let that woman make you think otherwise! I don't know your mother or Anna Lee that well but I do know they put way too much on you. Anastasia was never your responsibility—"

Ana cuts him off before he can continue, moving her chin out of his hand, "B*ut She Was*!" Her voice is raspy with sorrow, "She Was! She was my sister! I promised Daddy, I promised Mother, I promised Lee, I promised Myself! I knew this was gonna happen to her and I Did Nothing!" She screams at him, and shoves his shoulder roughly hoping it would change her mood but it doesn't, "I Let Her Die! I Let Her Demons Control Her! I Should Have Saved Her! I Should Have Saved Her!" Ana's screams are mixing with her tears as she starts to pound on his chest with her fists and Wren can do nothing but grab her. He pulls her into him from across the front seat.

"I'm so sorry baby," is all he could muster through his own tears. Seeing her cry out in so much pain and so much guilt made him weep. She sobs into his neck as the tears stream steadily down his own cheeks trickling through his goatee. He continues to mutter, "I'm so sorry baby. I'm so sorry baby." He repeats it over and over again as she cries uncontrollably into him. He doesn't even realize that he's apologizing. He knows he didn't do anything wrong but he's sorry that he can't do anything to change this moment for Ana. He knows that he has to just let her move through it and no matter what he has to be there for her.

So he is there for her.

Ana is able to cry and release all of her frustrations onto Wren. She stops weeping after the tears won't fall anymore. She moves out of his grasp and back into the seat. With a stuttered sigh, she takes her handkerchief and wipes her face. Then she looks at him, his eyes are a bit red, but she couldn't tell that he was crying too. He just looks exhausted. She takes the handkerchief, reaches over to him, and begins to wipe his neck and his jacket. Everywhere she had shed a tear on him. He grabs her hand to stop the motion, but then lets it go without saying anything. He just lets her have her way in this moment. He is so accustomed to taking care of her that this mild gesture the feeling of her touch is uncomfortable to him.

He finally starts the car just as the services must be finishing up. The mourners are dispersing and trickling back into their cars. He doesn't wait for anyone to come up to the door and ask how Ana is doing but pulls away onto the road leading out of the cemetery.

He drives for a while, down a long stretch of road, until his surroundings become familiar again. They arrive to Ana's house and she is asleep in the passenger seat. The day, her job, these last few weeks have definitely taken a toll on her. He gets out of the car quietly to make sure she doesn't wake up. He takes her keys out of her bag and unlocks her front door. Wren goes back to the car and opens the passenger side door. And just as he has done on so many drunken nights, he effortlessly scoops her out of the front seat and into his arms to carry her over the threshold.

Wren walks inside her house, kicks the door closed behind him with his foot and carries his love up the stairs to her bedroom. He lays her gently on the bed. She stirs a bit but doesn't wake up. He goes downstairs to lock the door and grab a glass of water.

He brings the water upstairs to her room where Ana is still asleep; at least he thinks she is. After sitting the water on the nightstand next to Ana, he walks over to his side of the bed and begins to undress. He kicks off his shoes to their usual corner, behind the door. He takes off his jacket, shirt and pants; laying them neatly over the back of a chair she has in the corner of her room, sitting at a desk. He sits on the bed contemplating if he should get in the shower or go downstairs to watch TV and let her rest.

Before he has the chance to make a move, Ana's arms are draping over his shoulders from behind him. He was so lost in his thoughts he didn't feel her get up and move. Her hands move down his chest and her lips slowly caress his neck. She can taste the saltiness of her tears that have stained his skin. He closes his eyes as he indulges in her supple lips brushing up against that spot just under his ear. He groans a bit but then murmurs, "We don't have to do this."

"I know, but I want to," she answers his thoughtful objection. That is enough for him.

He pulls her gently by her left shoulder moving her so she lays across his lap, looking up into his eyes. He holds her head so delicately leaning in to kiss her. His tongue, moving around slowly and deliberately around hers is getting her walls moist as she moves her knees up and down, and her legs back and forth falling deeper and deeper into the kiss. He wants to runs his fingers through her hair like he always does but the braid is in the way. Ana can feel his fingers aimlessly wandering over her hair and decides to change positions. She sits up and pushes Wren down onto his back, but he props himself up onto his elbows so he can watch her.

Ana stands, first taking her hair down, and then pulling her dress up and over her head. She unhooks her bra and cutely wriggles out of her panties. He can smell her natural scent and it's driving him crazy. He wants to be inside of her right now but knows not to rush this moment. His manhood is almost bursting through his boxers until Ana kneels down in front of him.

She grabs his boxers by the waistband and pulls them down toward her. He lifts up just enough for them to slide off without Ana having to struggle. His glorious shaft is standing fully erect waiting for her. He makes it jump, which always makes her giggle. He drops from his elbows and lies back waiting patiently. He feels a little chilly until he feels the warmth of her mouth wrapped around his penis. He lets out a moan of sheer pleasure as she inhales him into her mouth, allowing him to touch the back of her throat; testing her gag reflex. It appears as if she doesn't have one. All he can see is a mound full of crimson curls maneuvering up, down and around his penis. He closes his eyes as they roll toward the back of his head. He can feel his abs tense up as she slides her tongue up and down the underbelly of his manhood sucking it each way she goes. She even lets her teeth graze the tip ever so lightly. He hates the level of his need but the sensation is undeniable; it's insatiable. It makes him grab her by the hair hard, which is just how she likes it. He starts to grind against her face. As he holds her head steady, he moves in and out of her mouth just as he would her vagina. He fucks her face and continues to the point of where he's about to cum.

She reaches up above her head and grabs his wrist by their pressure points; squeezing them tightly. The pain and pressure of this technique forces him to withhold his climax and let go of her hair. Ana doesn't want Wren to finish in her mouth.

Ana moves her mouth off of his shaft leaving it dripping in her saliva. She parts her lips and fingers herself a few times while stroking him to make sure he stays hard. Wren is moaning and annoyed with the pain, but the softness of her hand massaging him back into his zone puts him at ease. Then he feels what he's been longing for since she started kissing on his neck. He opens his eyes to the crimson haired beauty riding him. She slipped his penis inside of her and they fit together like two puzzle pieces. She started off slow, rocking her hips back and forth, with her knees pinned down by his sides and his hands grabbing her around her waist. She is leaning forward using the cover above his head as her anchor to push herself back and forth onto him. She orgasms quickly, letting out a scream, looking up to the ceiling as if there were a God there making this climax the best one of her life. She looks back down to him, and her curls fall gracefully around her face. He bites his bottom lip looking at how beautiful she is, especially when she's coming. She continues to ride him as he uses one hand to push her upward, making sure he is fully engulfed. This position always gives Ana a sharp pain in her pelvis, so she leans back a bit further resting her hands on his thighs to make it bearable. She finds her rhythm again and continues to ride him stopping for a second or two, every so often, to prolong his ejaculation. His hands reach up grabbing her breasts, pinching and pulling her nipples as she rides him. She lets out a scream of passion and begins to speed up. He knows she's coming again. But he's had enough of her playing with him.

Wren moves his hands from her breasts to the bed pushing himself up and grabbing her back just as she starts to lose her balance. She wraps her legs around him as she now sits up, face to face, atop his manhood. He moves his arms around her to roll Ana onto the bed. He stands up over her and looks down to her with a menacing grin that makes her giggle. She can never take his mean glares seriously. He bends down, sliding his arms under her thighs and moving her all the way to the edge of the bed. He puts her feet up onto his shoulders and slides inside of her for the last time during this session. He pounds away into her pleasure making that noise...that *Thwop*...with every thrust into her as her ass smacks against his legs. Ana screams and comes again. He looks down to see her juices dripping down his shaft. The sight enthralls him, making him fuck her faster, deeper, harder until he finally locks his arms around her knees and succumbs to the intense pleasure that comes from being inside of her. He releases himself fully into her with a low and long growl.

"Oh shit," he exclaims exhaling and collapsing onto the bed next to her.

"Yes indeed," she replies panting. It was one of the most intense sex sessions they had ever had. All of the emotions from the day coupled with Wren just being there for her when she needed him made Ana all the more aware of one simple fact. She turns over onto her side and props her head up with one hand while stroking his chest with the other. He moves hair from her face as she looks him square in the eyes, "I love you."

"I know," he says with a smile, "I love you too."

She is relieved that he said it back and collapses back onto the bed. Ana ignores the fact that he was being a smart ass about it. She watches him get up from the bed and walk to the bathroom. He turns the shower on and at that moment she knows that he is who she wants to be with.

As Wren washes up; Ana isn't sure but thinks she hears someone knocking at her door. She gets up from the bed, looks around, and then decides to grab Wren's shirt that he had on today. She throws his boxers on, slips on her flip flops and scurries down the stairs to see who could possibly be at her house on a day like today.

She opens the door to see two familiar faces standing there. She grimaces while rubbing her forehead. Anastasia's arresting officer and the Assistant District Attorney were standing there on her doorstep.

"You have got to be fucking kidding me! What the hell do you assholes want?"

"May we come inside," the ADA asks her. The arresting officer is used to seeing her in Marshal gear but now Anabelle Strayer is standing in front of them in an oversized shirt, with her curly red ringlets tossed to one side over her head, and looking sexier than ever with an after-sex glow.

"Hell-Fucking No! You got two minutes to speak your piece. Go!"

"We just wanted to come by and pay our respects to you and your family. *We are* sorry for the loss of your sister during the unfortunate situation that she was in," the ADA begins, "and we know that this is not the best time but we kind of need your help."

"My help for what?" Ana questions growing increasingly agitated by their presence.

"Well, we know you have been privy to some information about the case, as far as an informant and the other officer that was involved in making your sister's arrest. And we really need to find the other officer's informant. We have a feeling that you know where and how to get in touch with her." The ADA tries to reason with her.

The officer interjects, "Besides you need to help us anyway! It's professional courtesy!"

"Oh now you wanna talk professional courtesy you son of a bitch! Mr. *Your favors are officially cashed out* ! I don't believe that you have the audacity to even think this was a good idea, on the day of Asia's funeral no less! You have got a lot of fucking nerve—"

Before she can continue cursing them out the ADA waves his hands in the air as a sign that he surrenders, "I know and I apologize for his abruptness. I came here because I knew I could deliver this message with a grain of salt rather than the sand paper he calls a mouth." the ADA chuckles uncomfortably by himself. "But we really need your help with this. The other officer is under investigation with Internal Affairs and won't cooperate with us any more without an attorney and a whole bunch of bullshit and red tape. We need his informant to come and tell us what she witnessed so we can actually vindicate your sister and get the guy responsible for putting her into our hands in the first place."

"*Aww* poor you, gotta actually do your job instead of setting up easily manipulated drug addicts to do your dirty work for you. But you know what I got something that can help you just wait right here please," Ana walks away from the door leaving it cracked and runs upstairs. She reaches for the bag in the bottom drawer of her nightstand and pulls something out of it before running back downstairs. Wren is just getting out of the shower and looks at her curiously with an eyebrow raised. He shakes his head and goes back to drying himself off. Ana returns to the door with a smile as wide as can be.

"So what do you have for us? Is it a tape, an address, or something we can use to get his informant?" the ADA asks with excitement impatiently . The arresting officer rolls his eyes, and sucks his teeth. His reaction is one that Ana has always detested.

"You know what asshole?" she says to the officer.

"What?" he responds to her with such a nasty attitude.

She pulls out a double sided dildo from behind the door, the object she took out of her bag in the nightstand, and tosses it at the cop, "The both of you can go FUCK yourselves!" She feels amazing having that moment above them and then being able to slam the door in their faces was just the icing on the Fuck Off cake. Wren comes downstairs, chuckling, having heard and saw the tail end of the conversation. The both of them look at each other and laugh as they hear the cop cursing from the other side of the door.

"Strayer!!! You miserable fucking cunt!"

Wren stops laughing when he hears that. He storms toward the door, moves Ana out of the way and opens it. Even though he was just in his boxers, his massive chest with the beastly wolf tattoo and the pissed off gleam in his eye shows he is not to be fucked with.

"Excuse me? What did you just say?" he questions the two men after swinging the door open surprising them that he was even there.

"Umm nothing," the ADA says, starts backing up, "I... uh...I think... he uh...had ...uh something to say...uh...but I...uh-... was ...just...leaving. Yeah, I'm leaving."

The ADA retreats back to the car they came in leaving an angry Wren there with the arresting officer; who also buckles under the pressure.

The officer stammers, "Nothing, I apologize...Umm...she threw a penis at me...and I got kinda distracted and was like *whoa,* is this a penis? And it was...so I dropped it...and umm...I'm sorry...I didn't mean to call you," he holds his hand out pointing to Ana who's standing behind Wren, "umm a miserable fucking cunt. Because it's quite obvious here...that you are not miserable...*and* you are not a fucking cunt, or any kind of cunt for that matter. I'm sorr—"

Before the officer can finish stuttering out his apology Wren tells him to go fuck himself slamming the door in his face. They both wait and listen to hear the officer walk away from the door. All they hear is him repeating to himself, "I shoulda brought my fucking gun! I shoulda brought my fucking gun!"

They both crack up hysterically, and continue laughing for the rest of what started as an awful day.

Chapter 13

Ana opens her eyes. The TV is still on, and Wren still has his arms wrapped around her. They had fallen asleep cuddling on her couch underneath a blanket. After the ADA and officer retreated, they decided to stay in watching movies and enjoying each other's company to try and forget all of the stress from Asia's funeral.

Ana sits up to stretch and yawn, slowly maneuvering out of Wren's grasp so as not to wake him. Wondering what the time is; she begins to look around for her phone. She finds it on the coffee table to see that it's a little after five in the morning. She picks it up expecting to see a ton of missed calls and text messages from "Eva," but there was nothing from her. She wonders why that is since Eva has been a nonstop nuisance since she left her at the spa that day. She shrugs her shoulders at the thought while continuing to scroll through her notifications. Anna Lee has called her a few times though. She knows that their mother was in a state of emotional turmoil, but she feels like Lee knew that's how their mother has always felt and she has never done anything to defend her. She continues to look at the phone contemplating whether or not she should return her sister's call.

"Call her," Wren grumbles in a barely audible request.

"Huh? Call who?" Ana assumes that he's talking about Eva but suddenly dismisses the thought.

"Your sister. You only have that look on your face when you're deciding whether or not to deal with your sisters." Wren moves his legs from off the couch to the floor, tossing the blanket over the arm of the sofa. He grunts as he rubs his hands through his hair and then over his face.

"I don't know," Ana's unsure if she wants to deal with Anna Lee compounded with their emotions from yesterday.

He exhales again, shakes his head, and gets up from the couch to start making his way up the stairs. Whatever conversation she needs to have with her sister, he doesn't want to be privy to. He decides to go back to sleep, but upstairs in Ana's bedroom. Just as he reaches the first step, someone knocks on the door. He stops, hoping that it was the cop coming back with his gun for a fight. The person knocks on the door again, and rings the doorbell this time too. Wren turns away from the stairs motioning for Ana to stay on the couch. He grabs the blanket off the sofa to drape over himself on his way to answer the door.

Wren opens the door to see Anna Lee standing there.

"Well are you gonna move out the way so I can come in?" she demands it rather than actually asking. Wren looks at the petite woman and moves out of her way without saying a word. Ana looks up from the couch to see who he's letting inside the house. She sighs and rolls her eyes once Anna Lee enters into the living room and cuts on the lights. Wren closes the door behind her and makes his way upstairs to let them talk.

"I don't wanna talk to you right now Lee," Ana fires off, "I'm still hurt from what Mother said and I just don't wanna be bothered right now."

Anna Lee completely ignores what her sister is saying to her and sits down next to her on the couch. Ana begins to notice the actual state her sister is in. Lee is still in her dress from the funeral, her face is clean of all the makeup she had on, but her eyes are red as if she hasn't slept in days. Ana's beginning to think this visit has nothing to do with what happened with their mother yesterday.

"Are you okay Sissy?" Ana asks suddenly worried why her sister is sitting in her living room.

"I don't know yet," Lee answers.

"What do you mean? What's going on?"

"Um, Jason hasn't been answering his phone or the house phone," Lee starts rubbing her knees and rocking back and forth, "He only ignores my calls when he's mad at me, and I swear since you came that day I've been on my best behavior." She raises her fingers in the air, motioning the signal for Scout's Honor.

Ana shakes her head at her sister asking, "Have you gone home yet?"

"Look at me Sissy! Does it look like I've been home yet? I took Mother home and stayed with her for the rest of the day. When she finally fell asleep, I called Jason, and the phone just rang. If he's mad at me, he usually sends it straight to voicemail. It never just rings and rings. Last time I saw him, he was rocking Bella to sleep and that was it. I tried to get some sleep but I couldn't. Something just seems off to me. Something is wrong!"

"Lee you're always overreacting. Calm down."

"Calm down! I am calm! That's why I'm here! I know that if it's a situation where he's mad at me, you being there will keep Bella occupied while we figure it out, or if something is wrong and I know it is, you're a cop," Anna Lee looks her sister right in the eyes. She's on the brink of tears and Ana can tell that she is legitimately scared.

"Okay, okay Sissy. Let me get dressed and I'll follow you home in my car," Ana finally agrees to go off of her sister's hunch. She runs up the stairs to get herself together. She explains to Wren what's going on. He asks if she wants him to come with them, but she tells him that it should be nothing and that she'll be back soon. He watches as she throws on a pair of jeans and a T-shirt. She grabs her holster and gun from the safe in the closet along with her vest.

Wren sits up, "Whoa, whoa, whoa... I thought you said this is nothing!"

"I think it is because my sister is *always* exaggerating the situation. But I'd rather be prepared," she says searching for the US Marshal jacket that she hates. She looks at Wren with his face full of worry and tries to ease his concerns, "Okay listen if you don't hear from me or I'm not back or on my way back here within an hour, then come to my rescue at my sister's house. I'm sure you've picked me up there at some point but I'll text you the address anyway." She walks over to him and kisses him on the lips. It's brief and soft, but still does nothing to put Wren's mind at ease.

"Okay," he agrees to her option. He watches as she rushes out of the room and down the stairs. He looks at his phone on the nightstand as it lights up with the text containing Anna Lee's address. He wants to go back to sleep but knows he won't be able to until she's back in bed with him.

So he waits.

Ana grabs her work bag and leaves her house; desperately wanting to go back home and lay in bed for another couple of hours with Wren. Anna Lee is already in her car waiting for Ana to get into hers to follow her home. Anna Lee takes off before Ana even has a chance to put on her seatbelt. She's speeding to get home. Ana is sure that Lee's fears are working their way into her mind and running amuck. Ana pushes her foot down on the gas to catch up with her sister. Lee is driving dangerously, and while Ana wants her to slow down she knows that nothing will make her do that. Thankfully enough they arrive to Lee's house without causing a five car pileup.

Lee pulls into her driveway with Ana right behind her. She gets out of the car and doesn't bother closing the door. Ana rushes out of her car, closing Lee's car door along the way, and up the pathway to the house. Lee is red-faced with tears.

Ana looks at her like she's crazy, "Calm the fuck down Sissy!"

"I can't," she starts whimpering, "I know something is wrong! I just know it is!"

"Okay I understand that but," Ana stops talking.

Lee doesn't know why she stops midsentence but looks at her sister's face and follows her line of sight.

"Lee did you open this door?" Ana asks her sister. Ana looks at her and she just shakes her head, speechless. "Okay Sissy look at me," Ana grabs her sister by the chin to get her to look into her eyes to try and calm her down. "I need you to take my phone and call Greg. Call as many times as you have to, every single number under his name until he answers and get him here. Do not," she snaps her fingers in front of Lee's face to refocus her, "Do Not come inside until I tell you it's okay!" Lee nods her head up and down rapidly while grasping Ana's phone tightly with both hands.

Ana draws her weapon and moves close to the open door. She listens for anything or anyone that may be moving around inside, but she hears nothing. She uses her shoulder to nudge the door open just wide enough for her to slip inside without making a sound. She steps inside the house, into the long hallway. The first room to her left is the living room. She peers inside but there isn't any one in there. The kitchen and dining room is further back past the stairs, behind the living room, toward the back of the house. She thinks of Bella, and moves up the carpeted stairs quickly. Bella's room is right in front of her, right above the kitchen, and next to the bathroom. She peeks inside first but doesn't see anything. She steps inside her room and opens her closet door. Nothing inside, she looks around the room, and the only thing missing is Bella's little backpack that she keeps her DVD player and headphones in. Ana exhales as she starts to believe this is a ridiculous idea.

There isn't anyone here.

She keeps her gun drawn as she continues to search the upstairs, but no one is here. It doesn't look like anyone has been here. All the beds are made and nothing is noticeably out of place. She shakes her head, holsters her weapon and makes her way back downstairs. She walks to the front door and is about to go outside to her sister but remembers that she hasn't checked the kitchen. She spins back around and moves toward the the kitchen. She draws her weapon, takes a deep breath, and moves into the open space.

"Ahh" Anna Lee's screams fill the house.

Ana is in shock as she looks at the bloody scene in front of her.

"Ooh My God! What...happened...to...him?" Anna Lee questions her sister barely able to speak through her tears. But Ana is in a trance, nothing was supposed to be wrong, no one was supposed to be here!

"Anabelle!" Lee shouts at her, "do Something!"

Ana finally snaps out of it and begins to move. Jason is duct taped to a chair in the kitchen, near the sink. He is in his underwear and has several lacerations up and down his body. He's been severely beaten and there is blood dripping from the cuts down the chair. It's beginning to pool around his feet. Ana moves closer to him inspecting the wounds. They all seem to be pretty shallow but there are a lot of them. She puts her fingers to his neck checking for a pulse. It's faint but it's there.

Ana checks the kitchen pantry, takes a quick glance into the backyard, and comes back to Lee who is crying hysterically.

"I t-o-l-d y-o-u," Lee stutters through her words.

"Sissy," Ana grabs her by the shoulders, "I need to try and wake him up okay? Go get me some rubbing alcohol and a warm washcloth."

"We have to help him... Help Him Belle!

"Sissy I'm going to but I need you to do this for me okay?"

Anna Lee leaves the kitchen to get the items Ana has requested. She returns a few moments later with a bottle of alcohol and a dripping wet washcloth. Ana knows she's compromising a crime scene, but she needs to know what's going on and where Bella is. She tells Lee to go outside to call an ambulance and keep calling Greg to get him here. She wants to keep her distracted while she can from the fact that Bella isn't here.

Ana walks over to her brother in law. She looks on the counter behind him and then into the sink. There are four different knives in it, and each are covered in blood. She knows that whoever did this took their time. She closes her eyes trying to wipe the imagery from her mind. She twists out the dripping washcloth away from the sink, onto the floor near the pantry, and then moves back toward Jason. Ana wants to cry but chokes back her tears as she dabs some alcohol on the rag. She wipes his forehead with it. It's one of the few spaces on his face that hasn't been cut. She hopes that the potent vapors help revive him. He stirs a bit and moans. She waves the open bottle of rubbing alcohol directly under his nose.

His eyes pop open and he begins screaming. "Aah...Aah...Aah... Please...Please don't hurt my baby!" Jason stops screaming and begins to cry. "Bella! Bella! Bella!" he won't stop crying out for his baby girl.

Ana bends down in front of him so he can focus on her voice. Both of his eyes are swollen shut. "Jason! It's Ana! It's your sister! I need you to stop and breathe for me."

"Oh my God! Anabelle! Where is Anna? Where is my wife? Don't let her see me like this! Please!"

"Jason calm down! I need you to focus right now and tell me what happened! Who did this to you and where is Bella?"

"They took her. They were waiting here for us! They wanted Anna too!"

"Who is they?"

"Some man and some woman! The woman! The woman was in charge! She did this to me!"

"Huh? How? Who are they Jason? I need you to focus!" Ana is getting increasingly aggravated because he isn't making any sense.

"We came home from the service, and as soon as I put Bella down on the couch to finish napping, I was hit on the back of my head. Next thing you know I'm in here taped to the chair." His mouth is swollen with a busted lip making it hard for him to speak without blood dripping out of the wound, "she said that you had been ignoring her even though you've been looking for her. She said that you have to go get Bella. She wasn't gonna take Bella, but Anna wasn't here so she had to. She had to make sure you stopped ignoring her. She said to-—"

"Eva?" Ana asks as if that answer doesn't make sense to her. But to her...it doesn't.

"Yeah! She said to tell you that Eva has Bella at the spa and you have to come get her alone. That's all I remember," Jason tells her in a defeated tone. He's exhausted and broken.

"But why?," Ana starts breathing rapidly, "I don't understand why she would do this! Why did she do this to you?"

"I don't know…I don't know," is all Jason can mutter. The paramedics finally arrive, rushing inside the house. The local police department isn't too far behind them. Ana's world seems to be crashing down around her. Everything begins moving in slow motion as the police move her away from Jason. She's answering their questions, but isn't there. Her mind is off trying to remember the exact location of that damn spa Eva took her to. She continues to absentmindedly answer the police's questions until Anna Lee comes in to tell them that she came with her and that's how they both found her husband.

Ana flashes her badge and tells everyone that she has to go and will be back shortly.

Anna Lee doesn't care that Ana is leaving, as she escorts her husband to the ambulance alongside the paramedics. They had cut him from the chair but had not yet removed the tape off of his actual body. They wanted to do that at the hospital as they were unsure how long he had been bound. Fortunately for Anna Lee, her blind worry for her husband is distracting her from thoughts of where her daughter is, but that doesn't last very long. You can hear her cries from inside the ambulance as they pull away from the house.

Ana is in a daze as she moves to her car. Flashes of her moments with Eva are in constant replay in her mind. The kiss outside of the bar.The amazing orgasm at the spa.The constant barrage of calls and text messages that she chose to ignore. She should have paid closer attention to "Eva."

Ana is oblivious to the action going on around her; even Greg as he pulls up and shouts questions to her from his car. Everything seems to be moving in slow motion. Wren had waited for her at her house, but when he didn't hear from her he made his way over there. He's already out of his car and walking up to Ana. He's talking to her, but she's so out of it she's ignoring him too. Her only focus is to get to that spa,she has to get to Bella.

Wren is getting frustrated that she won't talk to him. He shakes her to snap her out of the daze. Greg gets out of the car to go defend his partner. He runs up to the both of them and takes Wren's hands off of her, while flashing his badge in Wren's face.

Ana looks at the both of them before getting into her car, "I'm going to get Bella."

"What?" they both ask in unison. But Ana doesn't respond to them. She just starts the car, reverses down the driveway, and takes off.

Wren and Greg look at each other and then race to their prospective cars. They both pull off into the street hauling ass after Ana.

Wren follows close behind Greg, but somehow they seem to be losing Ana. So Wren speeds up, cuts Greg off, and moves up switching lanes until he gets Ana into his sights. They keep following her but she gets to the spa way before they do. They find her car but aren't sure which building she's in.

Greg parks his car in front of Wren's and gets out screaming, "Are You Fucking Crazy? Driving Like A Maniac! You Coulda Got Us Fucking Killed!"

"Well fucking around with you! Who the hell taught you how to drive?! Driving Miss Fucking Daisy and shit! Where the fuck is Anabelle?"

"Well there's her car," Greg points out.

"No shit Captain Obvious!" Wren fires back at him. He doesn't want his worry to cloud his instincts and his judgment, but at this moment he just doesn't have a clue where she went. Neither of them do. So they stand outside of their cars waiting for something to happen to give them some clue as to where Ana is.

Ana steps into the spa with her gun drawn. The receptionist desk is empty and there doesn't seem to be any sign of anyone in there.

"Bella?" she calls out for her niece. "Auntie Anabelle is here baby! You can come out......Please come out baby girl."

"Drop your weapon Officer Strayer," Nina says from behind her. She rotates the barrel of her gun into the back of Ana's head so she can feel the weapon.

"Eva?" she asks, "Where is my niece? I'll do anything you want me to but not until you give me my niece and let me get her to her parents."

"Shut up and drop your weapon! You saw what I did to your brother in law.Don't make me repeat myself and have to go to work on you."

"Please," Ana kneels down slowly and places her gun on the floor, "Please Eva, just tell me where my niece is."

"Your fucking niece is fine. She's already with her parents," Nina rolls her eyes still pointing the gun to her head. She kicks her Ana's gun across the tiled floor. "Take out your phone."

Ana doesn't want to move, "I don't believe you, I want to see her and I want to see her now."

Nina strikes Ana in the back of her head with the handle to her Glock. Ana screams out in pain and falls to the floor.

"I'm trying to get you the information that you need, and you're not fucking listening! Pull out your phone! You know that thing that I've been calling and texting and that you been ignoring, you fucking Bitch!"

Nina kicks Ana in the ribs while she's still down. Ana curls up in pain, and her phone falls out of her pocket onto the floor.

"Call your sister," Nina demands.

Ana does as she's instructed. Anna Lee answers on the first ring, with a voice full of tears, telling her that Bella is there at the hospital with them. She was conveniently standing outside the emergency room ambulance bay when they pulled up with Jason.

Jeremy and Nina had waited for Jason and Bella to come home after the funeral. They thought Anna Lee would be with them but she wasn't. After knocking Jason unconscious, Jeremy took a sleeping Bella to his car along with her movie pack, while Nina stayed inside with Jason. Nina tortured and beat him for hours trying to get him to tell her everything she wanted to know about Anabelle. He would have answered her questions, but unfortunately for him he just didn't know. Once Nina was satisfied, and Jason wouldn't wake back up, she left. She told Jeremy to wait for Ana to come and once she did, figure out which hospital the ambulance would go to and to drop the little girl there. Jeremy agreed and hoped that no one would see him in the act. Once he dropped Bella off, he ditched the car.

"Where are you Sissy?" Anna Lee asks her wondering where she went and why she wasn't at the hospital with them.

"I'm okay Sissy, I'll call you back," Ana hangs up before Lee continues to ask her a million questions about what's going on. Nina bends down and snatches the phone out of her hand before Ana gets any ideas.

"See I told you! I would never harm an innocent child! Now get up!"

"Okay, but you harm innocent adults?" Ana questions sarcastically.

Nina takes a deep breath contemplating whether her sarcasm deserves immediate punishment, but she delays her reaction to be addressed later.

"You're going to pay for that! Let's go Anabelle," Nina waves her toward the exit with the gun.

"Where are we going Eva?" Ana asks her.

"You'll see when we get there...Hands up," Nina pokes her in the back with the gun nudging her outside toward a car. Ana puts her hands in the air and continues to walk outside toward the street.

Nina doesn't expect to see Greg standing in the middle of the street looking around for Ana, "I shoulda known he would show up too."

"Greg look out!" Ana yells trying to warn her partner. Nina shoots Ana in the calf.Her leg buckles as she screams falling to the ground. Nina then begins firing toward Greg forcing him to jump in between parked cars. Nina sees his car and remembers it from the day at the bank and shoots two of the tires out. She doesn't wait for Greg to get up before running to Ana forcing her to get up and limp to a car she had bought just for today's events. Nina forces Ana into the driver's seat and makes her drive with her wounded leg.

"If you hadn't been such a fucking smart ass, you'd be driving with two good legs!" Nina yells at her.

Ana drives away from the spa breathing heavily to try and alleviate some of the pain. It isn't working. She drives past Wren who is now helping Greg get up from the street, and down the road. The two men look into the car, locking eyes with Nina and Ana as the women drive away.

"Fuck man! I knew that blonde bitch had something to do with this!" Greg yells.

"With what?" Wren asks him, still trying to get a handle on what's going on.

"With our investigation to find Nina Slade! She was with that Jeremy asshole! And now she's got Ana. I bet you she's taking her to see Nina. They're probably gonna kill her! Give me your car keys! Call my office and get them here. Tell them to trace my phone! I'm going after them!" Greg commands.

Wren is not easily swayed, "One...You can't fucking drive!"

The two men rush over to Wren's car, "Two, *you* call your office and tell them to trace *us* because I'm going with you to get her!"

Greg shakes his head but agrees getting into the passenger side of Wren's car. Wren gets in and turns the car on, "And three...she's not taking her to see Nina Slade. That blonde bitch *is* Nina Slade!"

Chapter 14

Wren is speeding through traffic, zig-zagging between cars, and breaking every traffic law possible to catch up with Nina and Ana. He sees Greg out the corner of his eye gripping the seatbelt and handle above the door. The look on his face makes him chuckle. Greg's face is painted with a look of sheer terror.

"Hey you think we should maybe slow down? You know before we hurt someone!"

"Seriously? What kind of cop doesn't enjoy a high speed chase? You're a U.S. Marshal the very essence of your job is *this* right here! *Chasing People!*

"We chase people, but never in a vehicle moving this fast!" Greg exclaims with a look of queasiness in his eyes.

"Please don't throw up in my car," Wren pleads as he slows down.

"I won't, now that you're doing the speed limit," Greg exhales and rolls the window down. The cool air helps to ease his motion sickness. "Why did you slow down anyway?"

"Because I don't see them anymore," Wren answers as he strains his eyes to see past the cars in front of him.

Greg exhales with a sigh of disappointment. He doesn't want to risk taking too long to figure out where the women went out of fear of what may happen to Ana.

"What do you think Ana meant when she said she had to go get Bella?" Greg asks Wren trying to figure out how the little girl could possibly be involved with the investigation.

"I have no idea. But you know how protective she is over her sisters. I can only imagine how she must feel about her niece. Maybe Nina, threatened the baby to get to Ana. I honestly just don't know but how about we ask her when we see her?"

Greg nods his head and then another question pops into his head, "Hey how do you know that the blonde is Nina?"

"Dude, seriously, I need you to be quiet so I can concentrate. I think

I see them up ahead. As long as she doesn't see us, we should be able to tail them and get Ana out of there," Wren dodges his question.

But Greg doesn't let it go, "I need you to tell me how you know who she is!"

"How about this is your investigation! You tell me who the fuck I am and how I would know who she is!" Wren snaps at him.

Greg looks at him with a raised eyebrow not understanding why he's so frustrated. He sits quietly for a moment going through his memories of the case notes. There weren't any other males listed that they should have questioned or looked into. Greg is thinking so hard to place Wren's face and how he can be linked to Nina. His brow is furrowing and a small vein is beginning to pulsate on the side of his temple. Wren looks over at him briefly. He imagines the gears spinning in his head and smoke coming from his ears. He shakes his head and continues driving.

After a while, the streets begin to look familiar and Wren suddenly realizes where they are going. Greg, on the other hand, is looking out of every window,clueless. He knows what part of town they're in, but he has no idea why Nina is driving out here. He doesn't see the car anymore, but Wren doesn't look worried which makes him a little worried.

"I don't see them... Did we lose them again?" Greg asks trying to see why Wren is so calm.

"I don't see the car anymore, but I think I know where she's taking her," Wren says calmly.

"Well! You plan on letting me in on the secret!" Greg is anxious with anticipation and curiosity.

"You'll see in a minute...matter of fact we're here," Wren pulls the car over to the curb and shuts the engine off. He doesn't say anything else to Greg and gets out of the car. He walks around to the sidewalk and just stands there in front of the building. This building has been a place filled with so many memories; good ones and bad.

Greg walks up next Wren and says something, but Wren is in such a trance that he can't hear him. His stomach is churning as he looks up at the office building. There aren't any letters across the top of the building anymore because it's been abandoned for a while now. It is set for demolition.

Greg can't figure out what the hell is going on, or why they're standing there just looking at an empty office building. His rage is growing with every minute that he stands there without any answers.

"Hey! You gonna tell me now what's going on? You seem to have a bit more information than I do right now!" Greg asks.

Wren doesn't say anything.

Greg continues to question him, "Hey Wren! I'm talking to you goddamn it! Wren! Wren," but this time he pushes and shakes his arm while talking him.

Finally Wren answers him, "Stop pushing me man! I hear you! And stop calling me that!"

"Calling you what?"

"Wren!"

"But that's your name! What else am I supposed to fucking call you?!"

"Only Anabelle calls me that... To the rest of the world my name is Darren... Darren Carnegie!"

The sound of his name nearly knocks the wind out of Greg as he now recalls several parts of the case file with Darren's name littered through it. Greg thought he was dead.

Greg looks at him and then back up at the building, "Oh shit! I thought you were dead! The reports said—"

Darren shakes his head, "I know what the fucking reports said! It says that I was shot! I was shot in the chest by that blonde bitch. And this is where she shot me!" He touches his chest remembering the surgeries, the physical therapy and the fourteen hour tattoo session to cover up his scars.

The two men continue to stand there looking at the empty shell of La Rouge Cosmetics.

"But how?" Greg wants to know how such a glaring piece of information could have been left out of the reports.

"Now's not the time for how! We gotta get inside there and get to Ana!"

Nina and Ana are on the top floor of the empty building. There aren't any cubicles, no carpet is stretched out from wall to wall; there is nothing left except for concrete and dust. Nina keeps nudging Ana with the gun in her back toward the large windows. Ana limps toward them, trying to look out and get her bearings as to exactly where they are. She's tired of walking, and her calf is still bleeding. She finally reaches the window and turns around to look Eva in the eyes.

"You need to talk to me Eva so we can figure this out," Ana begins to reason with her.

Nina rolls her eyes and shakes her head, "You just don't get it clumsy girl with the curls. You just don't get it."

"What am I missing? We had some amazing times and I'm sorry I can't be the woman you need me to be, but I can't be with you! I know I haven't been the greatest friend but with my sister dying and work—"

"HA! Work she says," Nina scoffs.

"Yes my job is very demanding so I couldn't and I wouldn't lead you on. I just had to back off completely! I have this case and I really need to focus…," Ana continues to try and explain her behavior.

"Focus is right! You are definitely off your game! Shit your entire office is!"

"What are you talking about Eva? How do you know anything about my office?"

"Oh Ana, Ana, Ana…what do you think your commander is gonna say when they find out? What do you think Gregory is gonna say when he knows what we've been doing together?"

"My personal life has nothing to do with my job! Now tell me what the fuck is going on! Why am I here Eva?!"

"You're wrong about that my dear because right now your personal life has everything to do with your job! Who have you been looking for Officer Strayer?"

"*What*?" Ana hesitates and starts looking around the empty space for the nearest exit. She's getting even more nervous about where the conversation is headed.

"Who… Are…You…Looking for, Marshal Strayer?" Nina asks the question again, emphasizing her words by moving the gun side to side but still pointing at Ana.

"Eva… What?" Ana asks her rubbing her head. She's hoping and wishing this is all just a bad dream that she needs to wake up from.

"You know for an enforcer of the law, you sure do act like you're hard of hearing! Come on, Ana,play this game with me. Pretty please," Nina requests in a high pitch voice mocking the voice of a small child.

"What game?" Ana raises her voice. She's on the verge of tears but refuses to let this woman defeat her. Nina approaches her. Ana backs away until the window stops her. Nina is so close she can kiss her. Nina nuzzles her nose against Ana's neck and chin. She runs her tongue from the tip of her chin, over her lips and across her cheek up to her earlobe; which she bites ever so delicately. The gesture forces Ana to turn her head, pressing her face against the window. She shivers with fear and disgust.

"*Please*," Ana begins to cry, "Just tell me what you want. Tell me why we're here!"

Nina lightly taps the barrel of the gun three times on the side of her head, "Baby, I just want you to think. Who do you think I am? You wanna know why we're here? It's because this is where our love began; we wouldn't be what we are to each other right now, if the things that happened here a few months ago didn't happen. They say the smartest answer is usually the simplest, it's usually just staring you right in the face. Or, it licks your pussy." Nina's smile is sinister as she moves the gun from Ana's head to between her legs. She runs it up her thigh and stops dead center pressing firmly so Ana can feel it through her jeans. Ana closes her eyes wishing that whatever is going on would just end.

"Have you figured me out yet honey?" Nina asks moving the gun up from between her legs running it over her stomach and under her breasts.

It finally clicks for Ana, as she thinks of what Jason said to her, " 'she said you've been ignoring her even though you've been looking for her,'" but she doesn't want it to be true. She bows her head in shame continuing to let her tears fall.

"Oh well *bra-fucking-vo*! You finally figured it out! " Nina claps while taking a few steps back.

"So, what ,Nina? So what happens now?"

"Mmmm," Nina delights in the sound of her name spoken off of Ana's lips. She's giddy that she finally put everything together. Nina jumps up and down with excitement like a toddler getting ice cream. She runs back up close to her. "Now you get to answer my questions."

"But wait, can't you answer a few questions for me first?" Ana asks trying to stall Nina. Ana sees Greg and Wren come through the stairway exit door. But the space is empty. There isn't anywhere for them to hide to try and get the jump on her.

Nina, however, is so consumed with her big reveal that she's oblivious to Ana's sudden mood change. She looks her in the eye, "No, no, I have the gun. I ask the questions."

She takes a step back from Ana, "So question number one is, How Stupid Do You Two Assholes Think I Am?" Nina moves quickly grabbing Ana by the arm and spinning her around. The bullet wound in her leg forces her to fall to her knees. Nina now has Ana positioned in front of her so she can look out into the empty space. Nina checks the clip, clicks it back into place and buries the barrel of the gun into Ana's crimson curls until it touches her scalp.

Nina looks out at Darren and Greg who are walking toward her slowly with their hands raised in the air.

"Very good fellas. That's right .Nice and easy. Come join the fucking party." She watches them never taking her finger off the trigger. "Okay that's enough! Now drop the gun and kick it over there," she commands motioning her head toward the opposite side of the floor. Greg does as he's told, placing his weapon on the floor and kicking it hard. The gun doesn't stop sliding until it hits the wall. Darren shakes his head thinking of how long it would take for either of them to try and get to it now.

"So what happens now Nina?" Ana asks turning her head up to look at her.

Nina jerks the gun in a way to tell Ana not to do that. Ana can feel the gun is tangled in her curls and looks at Greg with wide eyes trying to signal him that she's about to do something, but he isn't paying attention. She doesn't wait for him to get it, she moves her good leg back quickly and to the side swiping at Nina's ankles. The gun is tangled in Ana's hair and twisting her wrist at such an awkward angle. Nina lets it go as she falls to the ground.

Greg runs to Ana to help her up and out of the way while Darren runs to grab the other gun Greg kicked clear across the room. Ana stands up using Greg's shoulder as a crutch. She pulls the gun out of her hair with Greg's help. Greg takes the gun from Ana and points it at Nina. Darren walks up to them pointing the gun at Nina as well. Nina's smile is devious as she stares into the holes of each gun pointed at her. She moves off of the floor and onto her knees. She waves her hands in the air as if she's surrendering.

"I guess I shoulda checked to make sure you were dead huh?" she asks Darren.

Darren shakes his head refusing to speak to her. It's taking every fiber of restraint in his body to not shoot her dead on the spot. He looks over to Greg and Ana, wondering what they were waiting for.

Nina looks to Ana, "Baby I'm sorry we couldn't finish our game. But you still haven't answered my question." She looks to Greg, "What would you say if I told you I know what she tastes like?"

"Shut Up!" Ana yells letting her emotions take over.

"What?' Darren and Greg both ask her at the same time shifting their focus from Nina to Ana.

"It was nothing! It was a mistake! I didn't know what I was doing," Ana begins to reason with Darren more than Greg. She knows that it was an experience that would hurt him more than anything. She can see the look of disgust and hurt written in his eyes. "Wren please—"

"Don't! Not here! Not now! Get this bitch out of here before I kill her," Darren demands of them.

"Oh no you're arresting me?" Nina says sarcastically. "Do you think that's the best idea Anabelle? You know how much I love women." She flicks her tongue up and down rapidly at Ana. It reminds Ana of the amazing orgasm that magnificent muscle gave her. Ana limps over to her and smacks her hard across the face.

"Oh Yes! Now we're having fun," Nina yells with an excited gleam in her eye. Ana shakes her head resolving that she's not worth the paperwork of an ass whooping. Ana turns to go back to stand next to Greg. It's a mistake she would regret for the rest of her life. Nina springs up, removes a knife that's tucked inside of her waist band, and plunges it deep into Ana's side.

Ana screams out in pain grabbing Nina's hand that's trying to dig the blade deeper into her abdomen. Nina screams out with her in ecstasy, wrapping her other arm around Ana's neck. Greg and Darren look at each other and then look at Nina like she's a wild animal. Nina licks her lips. She can feel the blood seeping from the wound and down the handle of the knife. Her lust for the dark red liquid is exhilarating!

"You see, there is no feeling better in this world than to feel someone's life literally in your hands. That's why I love the knife. That pinch as it breaks through the first layer of skin, as it slides through the flesh, until it hits the bone. Hmm," Nina looks down at the knife and jiggles it a bit.

Ana cries out in pain grabbing Nina's arm that's wrapped around her throat. Nina pulls the blade out quickly and digs it into Ana's hip. She feels the blade lodge into her hip bone. She smiles widely, "Ah yes! That's what I needed to feel!"

Everything is moving so quickly and Ana is in so much pain. Darren knows that they need to get her help and soon, but he can't get a clear shot. Greg starts taking small steps away from Darren. Nina follows him, using the knife like a joystick to move Ana with them. She backs Ana up so she can keep an eye on both Greg and Darren. Ana is growing weaker by the minute. She thinks of how Jason must have felt taped to that chair while Nina cut into him over and over again. She probably screamed with joy. The thought makes her tears stream again. The guilt is setting in that they are all here because she was too into herself to see who this sociopath really was.

"Just hold on Ana," Greg shouts, "Stay awake! Back up will be here soon!"

"Oh is that what we've been waiting for?" Nina asks with a smile and a chuckle. "This is why I will always win! You guys trying to do things by the book! I will do anything for my survival and I can guarantee that my pockets are so deep that I won't spend a day behind bars. I'm crazy you know. My money will put me in an excellent institution for treatment."

Nina pushes on the knife, and Ana screams out in pain. "Oh I'm sorry baby. Just wanted to be sure you were still here with us to see what you have done. Yes, yes, yes this... is ... all your fault. You should have just let me be! You didn't have to come after me! You forced me to do this!"

"Just shut up! Shut The Fuck Up!" Darren yells at her. He's had enough of her banter, of her attitude. The worst part about it all is that she's right. She's going to get off with an insanity plea.

"No one forced you to do this Nina. You've killed people, and have tried to kill many others. You didn't have to do any of this! You shouldn't have done any of this!" Greg yells.

"Well I can't have you two assholes gallivanting around the globe looking for me! We're going to end this now one way or another. I'll be honest," she looks at Ana who's beginning to fade out of consciousness. She taps her face a few times trying to keep her awake. "I'll be honest Greg, one of you should have killed me by now! It's only gonna get worse from here."

"And you should have killed me that day you killed Benjamin," Darren says taking a quick step to the side firing off two rounds. Both bullets pierce Nina in the skull. One gets lodged while the other comes out clean on the other side of her face. Greg ducks to move out of the way of Nina's brain matter splattering across the floor. Nina releases the knife from her grip and her arm from around Ana's neck allowing them both to fall simultaneously. Nina hits the ground with a thud. Her cold dead eyes, wide open, with that damn smile still slathered across her face.

Darren runs to Ana just as she hits the ground. And as he has done on so many occasions prior to this day, he scoops his love into his arms. She's out cold. He wraps his arms around her thighs being extra careful not to touch the knife and cause her any more pain. He moves to the elevators without a second thought to Nina's dead body bleeding out onto the cold cement, or to Greg who's on his phone trying to secure the scene and get the forensic team in. Ana's red curls have traces of Nina's blood in them as they hang over his arm. He looks down at her hoping that he can get her to a hospital in time. He doesn't care how they got to this moment; he just wants everything to be okay.

He just needs her to be okay.

Chapter 15

Most days used to start the same for Anabelle.

She would wake up, hit the snooze on her alarm clock, and turn over to see who's lying beside her. Her long, lusciously soft, crimson red curls would cover her face and most of her pillow.

Today is different.

There is no alarm clock ringing. Anabelle is not lying in her bed. There is no one lying beside her. But...

Someone is stretched out in two chairs by the window in her hospital room. Ana smiles at Darren as he sleeps awkwardly in the chairs. She looks around for her phone but doesn't see it. She takes a deep breath in, but the pain is almost unbearable. She clutches her side, moving her hands over the bandages wrapped around her torso. Her breathing becomes shallow. She grabs her chest as the machines she's connected to begin to make all kinds of noises. The beeping wakes Darren up. He jumps out of the chairs immediately rushing to her.

"Are you okay?" he asks trying to figure out what's wrong. All Ana can do is shake her head "No," with her eyes closed and teeth clenched tightly together. He runs out of the room to go get help.

Darren comes back with a nurse and doctor following behind him. The doctor checks her vital signs with his stethoscope while the nurse checks the readings on the machine.

"Is she going to be okay?" Darren asks full of worry.

"Of course not! She was shot and stabbed," Greg answers him from the hallway. He has a huge bouquet of flowers and some balloons. He walks into the room, but his voice is not the one Darren wants to hear at the moment. Greg walks over to the window to set everything down just as the doctor is explaining to Ana some of the side effects of the several surgeries she had to have in order to remove the knife and stop the internal bleeding. The sharp pain is mainly a result of the soreness from her abdominal repairs. He gives her tips on breathing deeply but not to cause so much pain.

"It's going to take some time and some physical therapy, but you'll be okay soon enough," the doctor speaks with a hopeful smile.

"Thanks Doctor," Ana is grateful that he came in to talk with her. She looks over at the flowers and balloons Greg just brought in. "Is all that for little old me?"

"Yep, everyone in the office signed the card. Can't wait for you to get back," Greg says with a hint of sadness.

"What's wrong?" Ana notices the shift in his body language when he said that.

"Yeah, I saw that too. What's up?" Darren chimes in.

Greg sighs, "I'm not supposed to say anything but the commander is thinking about bringing you before the Disciplinary Panel. He thinks you should be relieved of your badge and your position. He knows that what we did was in the service of justice, but the basis on how we got to that point is questionable."

"My niece was fucking kidnapped! What the fuck was I supposed to do?" Ana yells at him trying to justify her actions with Nina.

Greg raises his hands up in the air, "Hey! That we all get and understand! But you were supposed to call me, or the commander, anybody! What you did was reckless and dangerous!" Greg continues his attempt to talk some sense into her, "and you damn sure weren't supposed to fuck the bitch! I mean come on Ana, we were in the middle of an investigation. You jeopardized everything we were working on."

"So you're agreeing with him? With them? You don't think I should be a Marshal anymore?"

Greg agrees with their commander. He doesn't think she should be a Marshal anymore. She needs the desk job more than he does right now, but that's something he doesn't want to say, "Listen I think you're great as long as you're not distracted. Just take a leave of absence, get yourself together and when you come back this thing should have blown over. If you take an unpaid leave, they might overlook your disciplinary hearing."

"Whatever Greg. I'll think about it," Ana is obviously frustrated and doesn't want to talk about the possibility of her losing her job any more. Greg doesn't want to talk about it anymore either, so he turns his attention to Darren.

"So Ana is good. We saved the day. I think now is as good of a time as any to explain how you got caught up in this."

Darren is standing at the window peering out into the hospital courtyard. He wasn't trying to be involved in their conversation. He doesn't want to be included but he knows that Greg will never leave him alone until he tells him what he wants to know. Darren runs his fingers through his hair as the memories flood back.

"After Nina shot Benjamin in the face, she shot me in the chest. The force of the bullet knocked me back, but it didn't take me out. I was fading in and out until Blake started crying hysterically. The sounds of her tears kept me awake. When she gained her composure she called the cops and an ambulance. When they got there, Benjamin was already dead. He was dead the moment her bullet entered his skull. I was in a lot of pain and could barely talk, but I was alive. When they got me to the hospital they said I have thick bones," Darren laughs a bit to himself, "And that the bullet had lodged itself into my breast plate. The worst part was that the bullet fragmented when it hit my bone, so I had to have several exploratory surgeries after the initial one so they could get everything out. Once it was all said and done, they released me from the hospital and I went back to Blake's house. She had decided that she was no longer in need of my services. I've been doing some security consulting for various clients, but I haven't done actual body guard work in a long time. I started physical therapy about a week or two after I got out and that's where I met you."

Ana smiles, "Funny how the world works. I guess you were meant to see things through to the end with Nina."

"But that doesn't explain why none of the reports said you were available for questioning or that you had even survived!" Greg yells.

"The reports didn't say I was alive because there were a few bodies that they had to deal with when they got there. They just took a roll call of who was shot. It was chaos and they weren't organized. They were busy questioning Blake and then took off to find the security guard who was sitting at the desk. They were supposed to question me once I was fully recovered but I think the case got passed to you guys before that actually happened. I was just a piece of evidence that slipped through the crack, Greg."

"Yeah, it was a lot of different angles going on in this case so I can see how you were missed," Greg concedes feeling satisfied with Darren's explanation.

"Case closed. Right guys?" Ana asks with a giggle from her bed. The act of laughter is a bit painful as well.

"Case closed partner," Greg agrees with a smile, "So when are you getting out of here?"

"They've been saying a couple of days. I'm gonna be on crutches for a while because of the damage to my hip, but they said my leg with the bullet hole should be good. I get to go back to physical therapy. But as soon as I'm out and home, I'll let you know. Okay partner?"

"Okay asshole I'll see you when you get out then," Greg curses at her with a laugh. He shakes Darren's hand before leaving the hospital room.

Ana is right, in just a few days' time, she's released from the hospital and Darren is there to pick her up. He watches the burly male nurse wheel her out to his car. The guy looks like he belongs on a Harley at some backwoods bar. Darren just laughs to himself as he gets out of the car to help Ana get in.

Once she's inside the car she turns to him, "Did you bring it?"

"Yeah I brought it," Darren responds by pulling out her duffle bag that she usually brings to work. "Do you want to make any stops before I take you home? Maybe go see Anna Lee and Bella?"

"No they're going to come over later tonight, but you can swing me by my office," she counters.

"Really? You want to go to work in this condition?"

"Yeah I just need to bring this stuff in, and talk to my commander."

"Okay," Darren shrugs his shoulders and drives off to her office. It doesn't take them long to get there. Once they arrive, he asks if she wants his help going inside. Ana declines his assistance as she struggles to get the crutches out of the backseat.

"Well at least let me help you out of the car," he suggests. She nods her head in agreement and waits for him to come around to her side.

He takes the crutches out of the trunk and then helps her out of the front seat. He asks her one more time if she wants his help to get inside the building. Again, she declines it. So he gets back into his car and watches her hop across the sidewalk and through the doors.

About a half hour goes by, and Darren is asleep, leaning on the steering wheel when Ana taps on the window to let her in. He unlocks the doors. She tosses her crutches in the backseat and takes her time to get back into the car.

"I don't know why you just won't let me help you," Darren complains, but he doesn't want to argue so he changes the subject, "So is everything good? What's going on about the disciplinary hearing?"

"There won't be one because I quit," Ana reveals.

"Huh? Wait…why? I thought Greg said that an unpaid leave of absence should be sufficient."

"It would have been, but as I talked to my commander I realized that the reason everything with Nina happened is because I have a lot of personal issues that I need to deal with. Until I can get myself under control, I can't be trusted with the responsibility of that badge. So as much as I loved my job, and as much as I hate admitting that any of these red tape superior types are right, I don't deserve to be a Marshal. Not like this."

Darren reaches over to hug her, but the pain is too much for her to lean all the way into it so they fist bump and have a good chuckle over that. He knows that the decision she made to take care of herself is one of the first steps to her making the changes she wants and needs to in her life. He starts the car so he can take his crimson curled beauty home.

It takes Darren and Ana a while to get used to him helping her into the house while she's sober. They bumble and stumble around a bit, but eventually he gets her upstairs and into bed. He puts her pain killers on the nightstand with a glass of water and kisses her softly on the lips. In that moment he knows that he wants to spend the rest of his life protecting and caring for her. He doesn't care about the decisions she's made before today. Her decision to quit her job solidifies his feelings for her and he's going to do everything in his power to make sure she gets all of the help she wants, and all of the designated dick she needs. He looks down at her with his mischievous grin.

"What's on your mind?" she asks with a grin to match his.

"Nothing, just thinking about our future together," he answers.

"Well tell me about it," she demands with a sensual smile.

"I will babe, as soon as I get back," he leans down to kiss her again.

"Where are you going?"

"I gotta go see Blake to tie up some loose ends, but then I'm coming right back here and I'm all yours."

"Okay," Ana pops some of her meds and leans back to get some rest.

Darren takes the drive out to the Redwood compound. Even though he and Blake have spoken on occasion, he hadn't been there since she told him he didn't work for her anymore. He pulls up to the gate, rolls down his window, and presses his thumb on the small plasma square.

Nothing happens.

He tries it again, but this time a male's voice comes over the intercom, "I'm sorry sir but all guests must be on the list to gain entry, and that square is for employee entrance only."

He pushes the talk button to respond to the new security, "I understand, but can you tell Ms. Redwood that Mr. Carnegie is here to see her." He waits for a few minutes and without another word from the little box the gates buzz and open up, allowing him to drive onto the property. It seems so different from when he was running things. He drives up the long driveway and stops his car in front of her door.

Blake is already outside sitting on the steps.

Darren turns the car off and gets out. He walks up the stairs and sits down next to her on the top step.

"So, I'm not allowed on the property or inside the house anymore?" Darren inquires of her.

"It's not that, it's just that every time I see you I have those awful flashbacks and I need to keep this meeting brief. I'm in a good space right now, and I want to enjoy it while it's here. How are you? How's your life outside of this?" She gestures with her hands to everything around them.

"It's going well. Ana and I are thinking about our future together. But overall things are well. How have you been holding up?" He knows that he will never stop caring about her and how she's doing. He will always be her protector in his own way.

"Things are getting better. Like I said, I'm in a really good space and I wish you two the very best," she says to him with a genuine smile.

"Thank you, I really appreciate you saying that," he looks at this woman who's been in his life for over twenty years and now he knows that it's over.

He doesn't want to upset her but he came there for a reason. So he leaves it up to Blake, "Maybe I should go and come back when you're okay to talk about Nina."

The mere mention of her name makes Blake sick to her stomach. She closes her eyes taking several deep breaths trying to let the air sooth her queasiness.

"No, it's fine Darren, say what you have to say so we don't have to talk about it anymore."

"Well as I'm pretty sure you've heard by now, she's dead. Everything that she did to us, to you, it's over. I was the one that pulled the trigger and took her life. I felt like I should be the one to tell you that."

"Thank you, Darren. I'll be honest and say that I'm relieved she's gone but deep down I know that if I had just took on the responsibility of raising her, none of this would have happened. Benjamin would still be here, you wouldn't have gotten hurt and I wouldn't have to demolish my father's building. No one needs to see that place of death and be reminded of the craziness that went on in there because of me." Blake looks like she's about to cry.

"I need you to listen to me right now!" He turns toward her making sure to look her in the eyes.

"What Darren?" she returns his stare.

"Listen to me. What's done is done! You had no idea of knowing what kind of person she would have become had you taken her home. If she still turned out to be bat-shit crazy, then who would be to blame? Do Not let what she said get to you! Do Not let her inside of your head! She is dead and gone. Every single thing *You* did... You did for her. You did it so she would have the best possible life. The Slades are wonderful people and Nina was still fucking crazy. So don't you dare let those thoughts linger ! I've done a lot of things in my life that were deplorable, but I have no regrets because I did what needed to be done! I did things that no one else would have the balls to do. So don't you regret anything you have ever done because no one can ever say that you weren't *LOVING NINA.*"

***

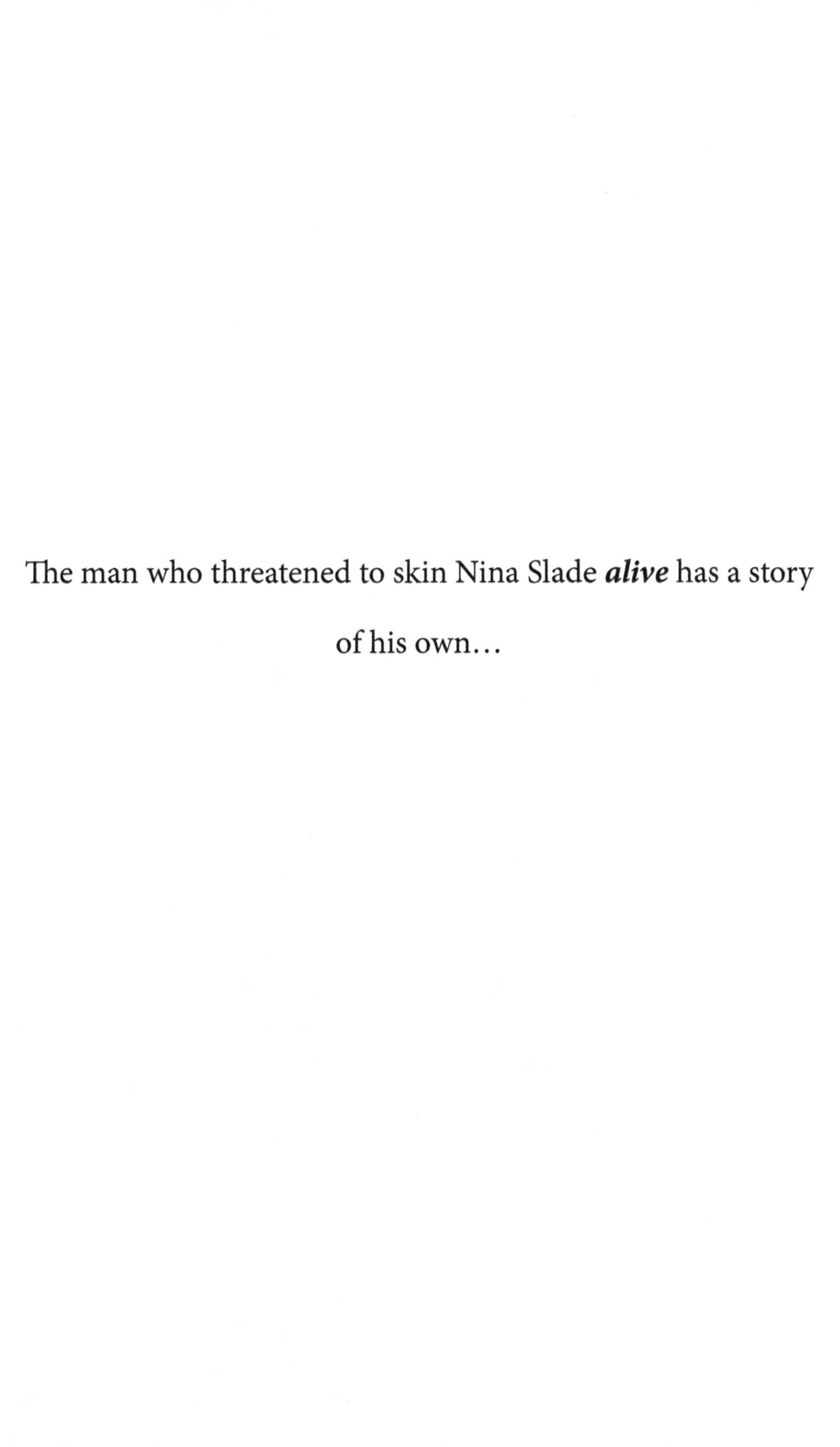

The man who threatened to skin Nina Slade *alive* has a story

of his own…

PLANTING THE SEED

The Moscow sun is bright. The afternoon is warm. Gabriel is a mere six years old. He stares out of the window watching the groundskeeper work in the garden. He wishes he could go outside and play.

THWAP!

The sound of his tutor's ruler hitting his open notebook startles him back to his lesson. Gabriel hates the ruler...the wooden ruler that never flexes...the stiff ruler with black numbers and tick marks.

"Again," his tutor, Yuri, commands. Yuri is tall and skinny. His cheeks are sunken in, partially covered by what appear to be sideburns that connect under his chin. The hair struggles to fill in fully in certain areas so he keeps it close shaven. Then there's the mole. It disgusted most people on first sight, but as you get used to Yuri you get used to it. It's about the size of a small pea, on his right cheek, just under the skin's surface. His nose is long which is perfect for holding up his gold rimmed glasses. He looks at Gabriel through the tinted blue lenses waiting for him to speak.

"Chtoby byt' kak vse eto na proval (Russian)," young Gabriel begins, "Per essere grande, bisogna essere disposti a fare (Italian) shénme suǒyǒu de rén (Chinese) ne sont pas en mesure de faire (French). No voy a mostrar debilidad (Spanish)! es wird keine Gnade geben (German)!"

"Na angliyskom yazyke!" his Russian tutor instructs he recite the entire canon in English.

"To be like everyone else is to fail (Russian)! To be great, you have to be willing to do (Italian) what most men (Chinese) are not able to do (French). I will not show weakness! (Spanish) There will be no mercy! (German)," the strength of the mantra is masked by the innocence of young Gabriel's voice.

"Very good, Gabriel. Your father will be pleased."

The compliment places a smile on the small boy's face. His tutor clears his throat and glares at Gabriel with wide eyes. It's a signal for Gabriel to adjust.

"YA proshu proshcheniya," Gabriel apologizes in Russian.

"In English," Yuri demands.

"I'm sorry," Gabriel repeats his apology.

"Why?"

Young Gabriel is on the verge of tears. He hates to disappoint Yuri. It is a direct reflection of disappointing his father.

"WHY!" Yuri raises his voice this time.

Yuri's tone scares Gabriel. He shrinks down into his chair as if he were trying to hide from the sound of his tutor's voice. He wants to cry but knows that it will only be worse if he does.

"YA proshu proshcheniya! YA proshu proshcheniya!" Gabriel pleads choking back his tears.

"ENGLISH!" Yuri demands again.

"I'm sorry! I'm sorry!"

"Your hands."

Gabriel hates this part. The six year old moves his notebook forward and places his hands palm down on the desk. He does it without protest.

The first time Yuri brings the ruler down across his knuckles, it hurts. It makes Gabriel cringe but he does not cry. It's the first time that he does not. Yuri brings the ruler down again across his little fingers. The pain is there again, but now Gabriel is getting angry so he refuses to cry. It makes Yuri angrier. He strikes him three more times with the ruler. His intensity increases with every strike. The sixth blow is the blow that breaks the ruler. It snaps just as it connects against the back of Gabriel's tiny hands.

Yuri screams in frustration still holding the broken shard.

Gabriel looks down at the broken meter stick lying on the floor beside his chair. He can see the look behind Yuri's shades. His tiny hands are getting stiff from the lashing. He knows that Yuri will pick it up before he continues with the beating. He watches Yuri bend down reaching for the other piece. Gabriel moves quickly pushing his chair back so he can hop down and grab it before Yuri does. He swipes the fractured wood and grabs Yuri by his tie.

Yuri is now face to face with his 3½ foot tall pupil. Something has changed within him. Suddenly, the mantra he had been forcing the child to repeat for these last four years was defined. The meaning of the words suddenly resonated with Gabriel. He looks Yuri in his eyes. He presses the jagged edge of the broken ruler against his jugular. Yuri swallows hard feeling his Adam's apple move against the sharp edge.

Young Gabriel has the demeanor of a grown man. He is mimicking the mannerisms of his father. The behavior that he has seen his father perform flawlessly, time and again, to get a specific result. He is calm when he begins to answer his tutor's question, "I must not smile, I must not cry, because Papa says it can be used to hurt me or to hurt him. I can't show my soft spots. My English must be perfect because Papa says so. My Chinese, my Italian, my Spanish, my German, my French…it must all be perfect because my Papa says so. I am struck with the meter stick when I do not answer fast enough; when I am incorrect. When I am not quicker than you, you will beat my hands with this stick." Gabriel pokes the wood into Yuri's throat.

Yuri feels a cold chill move down his spine as the small child still has him by the necktie crouched down to his eye level. He keeps one hand on the floor and one hand on the side of the desk to keep himself steady. Gabriel demands his complete attention.

"My hands hurt every week because I have not been quick enough. But today I beat you, and you will not hit me anymore. I will not show weakness. There Will Be No Mercy!" The shard of wood moves effortlessly as if it's an extension of his tiny hand thrusting the jagged edge of the ruler up into Yuri's chin. It just pierces the floor of his mouth scraping the underbelly of his tongue.

Yuri screams out in pain as the blood begins to pool in his mouth. It spills from behind his lips, dripping down his chin. He has the thought to spit in the child's face, but knows the wrath of the child's father will be much worse than the pain he is in now. He pushes Gabriel away from him forcing him to stumble and fall onto his backside. The small child watches as his tutor runs away from him in search for help. Yuri spits a crimson trail along the way.

That is what he gets for striking me...

Some are truly rooted in EVIL...

GABRIEL'S GARDEN

COMING SOON!!!

To all my readers

I thank you

xoxo

T.N. Jones

My beautiful daughter Sidney, my wonderful mother Bjae...keeping me focused on pursuing my goals.
Doug Brinson Jr.
Again I thank you and everyone else involved in this crazy plan of mine to live out my dream.